MW01119239

Trusting Again
in
Summit County

Trusting Again in Summit County

Summit County Series, Book 2

Katherine Karrol

Trusting Again in Summit County

Copyright © 2018 Katherine Karrol

All rights reserved.

ISBN: *9781729339275*

Publisher's Note: This is a work of fiction. Names, places, characters, and incidents either are the product of the author's imagination or are used fictitiously, and any resemblance to actual persons, living or dead, events, or locales is entirely coincidental.

Table of Contents

Chapter 1

Rutherford pulled Martha into his embrace. She tried to resist at first, but he held firm, looking deeply into her eyes.

"Martha, I've loved you since the day we met and I know you love me, too. Now that this blasted war is over and there will never be another like it, I want to marry you and settle on this land with you." Martha fell into his arms. "Yes, Rutherford. Yes."

"Yes!"

Rachel Stevens grinned as she closed her laptop. When she looked at the clock, she jumped up. *Oops!*

She dragged a comb through her hair, threw on wool pants and a sweater, and ran downstairs. Fortunately, her long hair didn't require a lot of maintenance and she wasn't much for makeup these days. That, along with the fact that she wasn't trying to look cute for anyone, least of all her date, made getting ready a breeze in a time crunch. Thanks to her books, time crunches were the norm.

"Sorry, Grandma. I was lost in a book and I didn't realize what time it was. What else do you need me to do to help get ready to go to Auntie Ev's?"

Grace Stevens chuckled. "You and your books. It's a surprise that there are any left that you haven't read. I put the rest of the dishes we're taking in the box in the kitchen. What time is Ben picking us up?"

Ben knocked on the door as if on cue and right on time, as usual. Good old Ben. Nice, reliable, dependable Ben. Boring Ben. Actually, boring was Rachel's favorite quality about Ben.

Boring men don't break hearts.

They drove the few tree-lined blocks to Evelyn Glover's home for her annual Thanksgiving gathering at a snail's pace. Ben drove like he did everything else: slowly and carefully. Rachel didn't mind; she just enjoyed the view as she looked past Ben to the landscape beyond.

She loved her little town, protected from the outside world by large forested hills on three sides and Lake Michigan on the fourth. She especially loved it in the fall, when the hills were covered in various shades of reds, yellows, and oranges. She took in the scene, knowing it wouldn't last long. Fall was rolling out more slowly this year, so there was more color left on the trees than usual and the faint smell of burning leaves hung in the air, but it was never quite long enough for her. It was a great day to spend with grandma and some of their closest friends, including Ben.

Rachel and Ben had fallen into a habit of spending time together over the previous few months. They had known each other through church and his work at the post office for years, but had gotten to know each other better recently at the book club Rachel ran on Tuesday evenings at the library. Ben always read interesting books and always had unique insights about them. Rachel loved discussing books with Ben because he often picked up on things most of the others didn't.

She enjoyed spending time with him and he was always a perfect gentleman. In all the months they had been spending time together, he had never once tried to kiss her or talk about a relationship, and she had never once minded.

Rachel had had a heart-pounding, intoxicating romance once, charmed by a boyish smile, dirty blonde hair and light blue eyes, and had been burned badly enough to never want to try it again. It was enough that the memories of that relationship invaded her dreams. She didn't want to think about it or risk falling in love like that in real life again. *Above all else, guard your heart; for it is the wellspring of life.* Sure, her friends said she took the verse to the extreme, but still. It was Biblical. *There's no arguing with Biblical.*

She had all the romance she needed right at the tip of her fingers, anyway. She used to have to carry books around to get a fix if she wanted one, but now all she needed was an app on her phone. Romance was just a tap away, and no one got hurt.

Chapter 2

Derek Cooper looked up at the stop sign just in time to see the back of Rachel's dark blonde hair as she rode in the passenger seat of Ben Peterson's car. He felt the vein throbbing on the side of his neck as he imagined her looking adoringly at Ben the way she used to look at him.

"They're spending *holidays* together now? Are you kidding me?" He looked up toward heaven with a look meant to convey his displeasure to God. "Seriously, You couldn't have timed that a little bit differently?"

Brutus looked at him and whimpered.

"You get it, don't you Brute?"

How could they be spending Thanksgiving together? Is it really that serious?

He thought back to the last time he was the one driving her to Evelyn's house on Thanksgiving. They were laughing as she teased him about what she was getting him for Christmas. She kept saying that she was going to start buying things they would need later for their wedding so they could be practical.

"I'm going to get you a bunch of craft supplies so you can start making the decorations now. Since you're the artistic one, you're in charge of those."

"I'm not sure you want me in charge of that. My art is pretty much limited to canvases."

"You're not just a painter, Derek; you're an artist. You can make something beautiful out of anything." She always looked more serious when she talked about his art.

He reached over for her hand. "The most beautiful thing in that room is going to be you."

She had smiled and blushed, as she often did when he complimented her, and continued on with her Christmas gift ideas. "And I'm going to get you a calendar so you know exactly how many days are left until the wedding."

He smirked at her. "I already know how many days are left until the wedding."

They said in unison, "Too many!"

Suddenly she started giggling. "Maybe I'll get you a wedding veil for Christmas. You can use it when I visit you at school to cover that awful picture of me you insist on keeping on your desk, and I can use it later when I walk down the aisle."

"I love that picture; it's the first one I ever took of you. And I don't ever want your face covered. I love your beautiful brown eyes and your bright smile and don't ever want them to be covered up." More blushing.

"You'll have the rest of your life to look at my face." She smiled as she leaned over and kissed his cheek. "And I have the rest of my life to look at yours."

"Okay, I'll make the decorations if you want me to. But I still get to be in charge of the honeymoon, too. I already know I'm getting us a new blanket for our picnics in front of the fireplace in the little cabin. We can't very well take that ratty old one we use now."

"I love that blanket! It's been there for every one of our picnics and it has sentimental value." She smiled. "I even like the corner where Brutie chewed it when he was a puppy. You know what we do need, though. We're going to need our own picnic cooler because we won't have access to the old one at your parents' house."

"I like that old cooler. It has sentimental value too. Maybe I'll ask them to give it to us for a wedding present."

She laughed. "Perfect."

When they arrived at Evelyn's, he turned and looked at her. "I wish we would have taken a longer way here so we would have more time without other people around. Seriously, though, Rach, before we go in there, I want to tell you that what I'm most thankful for is you. You make my life better by being in it and I can't wait to marry you."

"Hey, you took my line!" She playfully hit him on the arm, but then took his hand and held it in hers while she looked into his eyes and her expression grew serious. "Derek, I couldn't be more thankful for you. You make me feel loved and safe and like nothing can ever hurt me."

She leaned over and kissed him the way that only she could and he wished the wedding they were planning was a few months away instead of two years.

Derek was jolted out of the memory when he felt the tears rolling down his cheeks and realized he was still sitting at the stop sign.

Having to see her around town always stung, but having to see her tool around with her new boyfriend *on a holiday* was just too much. It was just one more reason to hate this town and living in it.

He was completely blinded to the beauty of the town he once loved by this point. The hills that surrounded it on three sides and Lake Michigan on the fourth used to make him feel like he was living in a painting. Now they just made him feel boxed in, *trapped*. Summit County in general and Hideaway in particular felt like his own personal torture chamber.

It had been three and a half years since he'd somehow messed everything up, forfeiting his future with her. It had been two and a half years since he'd been back in this stifling place, having to see her go about her life so easily without him. Meanwhile, he felt like his life had stopped; he was just existing and that just ticked him off. It seemed like everything ticked him off these days.

He was already in a terrible mood because he was on the way to his parents' house for Thanksgiving. Today, instead of celebrating a holiday, it would be just another day spent talking about the business, arguing about the business, and

Dad telling him and his brother about the way things used to be. *Oh, joy.*

At least Clayton would be there to commiserate with. They usually tried to find chores they could do to help Mom out – preferably outside, where they could be away from conversations with Dad. It was bad enough that he had to be with him 45 or 50 hours a week in the office feeling like he wasn't measuring up and having his ideas shot down; he really didn't want to hear it on Thanksgiving.

He looked at Brutus. "I wish I would have woken up with stomach flu this morning."

Chapter 3

Evelyn's big, beautiful Victorian home with its antique furnishings always took Rachel back in time. She had an eye for style and the ornately carved wood, tufted velvet, damask and jacquard, all in rich jewel tones, worked together to make Rachel feel like she was stepping back into history every time she crossed the threshold.

There was no place Rachel enjoyed more than history. She spent hours as a child devouring historical fiction, then as she got older, she expanded to include biographies and historical accounts of major events.

Being from Summit County, she was *of course* a huge fan of Bruce Catton's books about the Civil War. He had grown up a few miles away and was a local hero of sorts, at least for the older generations and regulars at the library. She often drove out of her way to pass by his former home and imagined him in there writing.

She looked at Evelyn's fireplace and pictured Rutherford and Martha dancing in front of it, unable to break each other's gazes. *Wrong time period, history major.* She chuckled at the thought of the Revolutionary War-era characters in the elegant Victorian parlor. "Rutherford, now that you've survived the war and the disease that went with it and don't have to live in a crowded tent and ration food, come sit on the velvet loveseat with me and try these new fangled delicacies called Candy Corn."

The day was fun, spent visiting, eating inordinate amounts of food, catching up with old friends, and playing Euchre. She loved the annual Thanksgiving meal; Evelyn and George Glover had started opening their home to friends many years before, and Evelyn had continued it after George died.

Rachel started going after she moved in with her grandmother when she was a young girl after parenting had become too much for her struggling mother. She hated the gatherings at first because she felt shy and out of place, but she grew to love the annual event as she got to know people in town and started to feel as if she belonged there. It was there that she got to know the two girls who would become her best friends.

There was always a different mix of family and friends, old and new. Sometimes guests at the Glover's bed and breakfast even joined in. Some of the Callahan family was there as always, although this year Brianna, the youngest Callahan and one of Rachel's best friends, was spending Thanksgiving with her boyfriend's family in Ohio. Rachel was happy that Brianna had found love, but hated the idea that she may move away permanently if she got married. It was bad enough that she and Shelby, Rachel's other best friend and Evelyn's niece, were both still in college and were only home for holidays and summers, if that. Having neither of them there cast a shadow on the day, but shadows had been hovering over her days for three and a half years anyway, so she had gotten used to it. Some of the Huntleys and the Burgesses and some friends from church were there, and Emily Spencer, Evelyn's guest-turned-boarder, had joined in as well.

There were enough people in the room that when the Lions game got near the end and they had a chance to win, all eyes went from the various game tables to the TV and no one noticed her sneak away to the small library.

She could sit in there for hours and sometimes did just that. Her grandmother and Evelyn were lifelong friends and when Rachel moved to Hideaway, Evelyn had become an honorary aunt. Rachel's love for this room in particular started when she accompanied her grandmother to Evelyn's for Bridge Club when she wasn't in school. They played their game and Rachel read Evelyn's books. It was Evelyn and her grandmother who had introduced her to Bruce Catton's books, and they had even made a big event out of it the first time they drove her past his former home.

It was this room that fueled her budding love for reading and this room that inspired her desire to always be surrounded by books and to get lost in other peoples' lives. She had learned at a young age that books took her away from real life and never let her down or hurt her. History books, in particular, didn't have surprises that turned worlds upside down. She sat in there with her eyes closed and inhaled the smell of leather, wood, and other people's stories.

When she heard loud cheering followed by the sound of high fives and back slaps, she figured the game was over and the Lions had somehow won. She never really understood the excitement of watching other people play sports, but liked the cover it gave her to sneak away for a moment of quiet. She joined the group as they headed toward the dining room as if she had been with them all along. *Introvert survival strategy #457.*

The Thanksgiving meal was filling and delicious, as always, and she enjoyed watching Brianna's brother Joe and Emily try not to get caught staring at each other. It was obvious that they had a secret interest in each other that they had not shared *with* each other and it was highly entertaining watching them try to sneak glances at each other without letting the other notice. It was as if someone choreographed their gazes and Rachel imagined a symphony playing in the background.

Synchronized peeking; this is my kind of spectator sport. She imagined them in one of her books and wondered how long it would take for the characters to admit they liked each other.

The cleanup after the meal was even fun, with Ben, Emily, Joe, and Mitch Huntley sharing the task and laughing together. Her spectating took on a new level as she watched Joe and Emily get nervous and blush when they got too close to each other while they were packing up leftovers and doing dishes.

It warmed Rachel's heart to see Joe interested in someone again. He had always been sort of like a big brother to her and it was heartbreaking when his wife died on the day she gave birth to their daughter a couple of years before. Rachel had always prayed that he would find someone again and hoped this was it. He was one of the few really good men she knew and she wanted him to be happy. She had always hoped to find a man as honorable as him. She thought she had found one, but it turned out she was wrong.

She looked over at Ben. *Nope, no spark there. Thank God. I'll keep my romance safely confined to my books, thank you very much.*

When Ben took them home, he brought the box of food that somehow seemed heavier than before the meal into the kitchen and helped Rachel put things away while her grandmother went upstairs to take a bath and go to bed. When they had put away what was staying there and put what was going to Ben's house in a bag, she walked him to the door.

"I'm glad I took Evelyn up on her invitation to go there today. I really enjoyed myself and it was nice to be with friends while my family is out of town. I even sort of enjoyed the few minutes of football that I watched." He gave a quiet laugh.

"I'm glad you came, too, and thank you for the ride." *And I enjoyed the football game, too. From the library.*

After he left, she thought again about the day and her mind drifted back to Joe and Emily. She still loved watching romance from afar, even though she avoided it like the plague in her own life.

Her mind involuntarily returned to the last Thanksgiving she spent with Derek four years before. They had spent part of the day at Auntie Ev's and part at his parents' house, as usual. It had been a day filled with laughter and fun and romance. *All* of her days with Derek had been filled with laughter and fun and romance.

Since they were for all intents and purposes engaged, there was no need to hide glances or try to stay away from each other. In fact, they had spent the day finding excuses to get away from the others so they didn't have to share each other. They made the tenth-of-a-mile drive from one house to the other take 45 minutes, took Derek's dog Brutus on more walks than he needed, and stole kisses and giggles in the pantry while they were cleaning up the meal.

She had never smiled or laughed so much as she did when she and Derek were together, and he was the person she got the most comfort from when her heart was broken again by her mother's situation or she was conflicted over something. He always had wise and encouraging words and bear hugs and always prayed for her, and she tried to return the favor to him. They were a perfect match, or so she thought.

She needed to get away from the memories; they felt too good and hurt too much at the same time. She had tried for three and a half years to convince herself that the only feelings she still had for Derek were anger and contempt, but she hadn't been able to, just as she hadn't figured out a way to kill the longing she still had for him and for what they had together

Chapter 4

Derek was glad the day was over. He tossed his keys on the counter in the small kitchen of his rented house and proceeded to the living room to see what was on TV. He didn't really care what was on; he just wanted something to stare at that didn't ask anything of him. He collapsed into the old recliner and settled on a repeat of *The Big Bang Theory*.

The day with his family had been exhausting. He tried to avoid shop talk, but as usual, his father brought it up. Derek missed the days when his dad could put the business on the back burner on holidays. On holidays and Sundays, Derek and Clayton used to *have* a dad. Now that the business was taking the hit that all small businesses were taking because of online competition, he was consumed. Brutus proved helpful, as he once again 'needed' a few walks throughout the day.

Derek empathized with his father's frustration. He would probably feel the same way in the same situation. Building a successful business from the ground up was hard work and he had paid his dues; the whole family had paid. He'd had to miss a lot of Little League, soccer, and football games because he was trying to keep a roof over their heads and build a future for them. He could relax and have fun when he wasn't at work, but the possibility was always there that the phone could ring at any minute with some type of problem that only he could solve.

He had tried his best to be a good business owner and boss. When there was a slow month, it was he who didn't get a paycheck because he wanted to make sure his employees did. He was a good man, a good man who was so consumed by the weight of his responsibilities that he had become almost impossible to be around.

It was always his dream to have Clayton and Derek take over the agency, and he was trying hard to make that happen. The problem was that in order to pass something to someone else, one must let go of that thing.

Clayton and Derek saw the problems the agency was facing. They were the same problems every small business faced. The world had changed since their father had put out his shingle. The internet wasn't a thing then, and customers went local when they needed something. Now instead of talking with their local insurance person, they were opening their computers, or even worse, opening an app on their phone. Clayton and Derek had ideas about how to continue to compete and how to embrace technology while still providing personal customer service, but they were shot down, seemingly because they couldn't be described with the phrase, "This is how we've always done it."

It occurred to him that maybe he needed to reconsider his life choices. In particular, he needed to reconsider where he was going to live for the rest of his life and what kind of work he wanted to do. He wanted out of Hideaway more than he had even admitted to himself. Between seeing Rachel and Ben on their way to bond over turkey and cranberry sauce and arguing with his father about work, he was feeling like he couldn't breathe any more.

He pulled out his laptop and started looking at job posting sites. *Looking can't hurt, right?*

Chapter 5

Rachel loved the day after Thanksgiving at the library. It was always quiet because everyone who lived in Hideaway was in Traverse City trying to get Black Friday bargains. Quiet days were her favorites because they gave her more chances to look out the picture window at the small bay and the large hills beyond it. Those were good days for daydreaming and thinking. They were also good days to do her own reading and research without being interrupted. It wasn't that she disliked working with the patrons; she liked it very much. She just liked the break from them too.

Emily came in through the door with a big smile on her face. *Mmm hmm. No surprise there after what I witnessed last night.*

"Hi Emily, no big shopping today?"

"Ugh, no way. I've got some end-of-year reports that I want to get a leg up on so I won't have to deal with them when the Christmas festivities are going on. I'm going to go into my usual corner and take advantage of the extra peace and quiet by digging into my spreadsheets."

Rachel smiled. "Sounds like a perfect way to spend Black Friday."

Emily had become a regular at the library as soon as she moved into town because she used the Wi-Fi and the table in the corner for her bookkeeping business. They had been friendly and Rachel was happy to see her start attending First Community Church a few weeks after she moved to town. Rachel didn't have a lot of close friends – by design – but Emily was approaching the line between acquaintance and friend. She had a trustworthy way about her. In Rachel's experience, that was not all that common.

It was strange not having Shelby and Brianna there on Thanksgiving this year. This was the first year that neither of them had come home for the weekend. Shelby would be moving back to Hideaway from Tennessee after her graduation in December, and Rachel couldn't wait to have her back in town. She missed having a confidant locally and was glad she would have at least one of them back. Brianna still had another semester of graduate school in Ann Arbor and wasn't sure if she was moving home or not, thanks to the job market and her boyfriend. *Thank you, Lord, for group texts and conference calls.*

Rachel was thankful for her friends. She had only ever extended enough trust to confide in four people in her life. Her grandmother, Shelby, and Brianna had been worthy of that trust; Derek was another story.

She thought about trust and secrets. She had a whole box of unshared secrets hidden away in her closet and more in a folder on her computer; even Shelby and Brianna didn't know about them. They were going to stay secrets for a very long time, maybe forever.

Chapter 6

Derek woke up with a stiff neck and a headache to beat all headaches. *Why do I feel hung-over when I didn't have anything to drink last night? What was in that pumpkin pie?* When he awoke fully and realized the position he was in, slumped in the old recliner with his laptop dangling precariously at the edge of his leg, he had his answer.

He had fallen down a rabbit hole while looking at job postings 'out of curiosity' late into the night. The rabbit hole got deeper as he saw jobs that he qualified for . . . and *wanted*.

He got up slowly, turned off the TV, let Brutus outside, and headed toward the shower. The hot water beating on his neck gave him the relief he was seeking, and he made some coffee and sat down with his Bible and journal.

"Lord, what am I supposed to do? I can't imagine this is Your plan for any of us. My family is being torn apart and I don't know what to do to stop it. Please help me see what to do. I hate my job, I hate living in this town, I love my dad but hate having him as my boss. More than that, I hate not having my *dad* anymore. Please give me direction, Lord. Should I just walk away? I need something to hold on to here. It's bad enough that I have to see Rachel happily going on with her life without me. I just need *something*."

He paused as he swallowed hard. "Lord, maybe the something I need is another job in another place. Dad doesn't like any of my ideas and Clayton can handle the business on his own whenever the time comes for Dad to pass the torch. Clayton actually *likes* selling insurance and is much more invested in the business than I am. Dad even listens to him occasionally. I don't care that it's supposed to be half mine someday. Part ownership in a business isn't worth this misery. It isn't worth breaking up a family. It isn't worth turning into an angry, miserable person. I don't want to become what I'm becoming."

He went to the kitchen and splashed cold water on his face before filling his coffee cup again. He was headed toward his computer to start updating his resume when Mitch appeared, banging on the kitchen door.

"Derek, Clay has been trying to call you all morning. Your dad had a heart attack a few hours ago. Get dressed and I'll take you to the hospital."

The 40 minute drive to the hospital in Traverse City would have taken two hours on the snowy and busy Black Friday if Mitch didn't know the country roads as well as he did. *Holiday shoppers are going about their business like nothing has changed in the world. Meanwhile, my world just cracked open and swallowed me whole.* He tried to shove aside the guilt of looking at other jobs and thinking about leaving town.

"Thanks for bringing me, Mitch." Mitch was a good friend of Clayton's and was a great person to have on speed dial in times of crisis.

"I'm glad to do it. I've got to get back to the hardware store so I can't stay, but I didn't want you to have to drive here after hearing the news. I don't know how long your dad will be in the ICU, but if you need me to bring anything to you or to do anything, just call. Zack can watch the store for me. I'll go let Brute out in a while and will check in on you guys later today if I don't hear anything." He dropped Derek off at the main entrance and headed back to Hideaway.

Derek took a deep breath and looked up at the entrance to the hospital. "Here we go, Lord. Please heal my dad. Just please heal him. Give me a chance to tell him I love him and I'm sorry for –" He choked back the words and the tears, took another breath, and crossed the threshold into the lobby. He should have been used to doing hard things alone after three and a half years, but for the millionth time since he'd lost Rachel, he felt her absence as if it were his arm or leg that was missing.

The Intensive Care Unit was a strange place. The only sounds came from machines and the distinct smell was not like anything he was used to. Fortunately for him, he hadn't spent much time in hospitals, let alone Intensive Care Units.

He hoped he and his family didn't have to spend much time in this one.

He reached his father's room and found him in a deep sleep. His mother and Clayton were sitting in uncomfortable-looking chairs and staring at screens full of graphs and numbers. They both got up and hugged him tightly. Both looked worn out.

"I'm sorry, I fell asleep watching TV last night and my phone died. I didn't know you were trying to call."

"It's ok, brother. I'm just glad Mitch was available to go get you."

Derek looked at his father lying in the hospital bed with tubes and wires attached everywhere. He looked so old and small and vulnerable, not like the man who Derek had loved and looked up to his whole life. His skin looked grey and his breath was slow. *Please, Lord. Please let him be ok.*

His mother placed her hand on his shoulder and spoke. "You just missed Dr. Wagner. He said the surgery went okay. They put in a stent, which took care of the blockage. They have him sedated for now so that he can rest without feeling pain. If all goes well today, he should be able to be moved to the step-down unit tomorrow." His mother was an amazing lady. Carol Cooper handled crises better than anyone he knew.

"Why don't we give him some time to rest and go down to the cafeteria for a bit? I could use a cup of coffee and you boys are probably ready for some food." Mom seemed to think they were still the always-hungry teenage boys she raised. Just as he started to chuckle over that, his stomach growled. *Mother knows best.*

"Can I meet you down there? I want to sit with Dad for a minute."

He carefully took his father's hand and just held it. He brushed his graying blonde hair back and kissed his forehead. "I love you, Dad." He couldn't form more words so he squeezed his hand and walked out, taking one last look at him as he walked through the door.

Chapter 7

One stereotype about small towns was true: word traveled fast. Rachel and Grace were just about to sit at the dining room table to eat dinner when the telephone rang. Grace's smile instantly fell when the person on the other side of the line started talking. *Must be a prayer chain call.*

"Hi, Sue. How are y– . . . Oh, no. When? . . . How bad is it? . . . Oh, thank God. How are Carol and the boys doing? . . . Yes, we will pray right now and will keep it up until told otherwise. I'll call Evelyn right now. Ok . . . Uh-huh. Bye, Sue."

The knot that had formed in Rachel's stomach when she heard the phrase 'Carol and the boys' only grew when her grandmother hung up the phone and turned to face her. The look on her face confirmed Rachel's fear. *Something happened to Derek's dad.*

"Ed Cooper had a heart attack early this morning. It was touch and go for a while, but he's stabilized. He had some type of procedure and he'll be in the hospital for at least a few days. He's still in the ICU now." Rachel could only stare and nod.

"Carol and the boys are doing ok. Derek is ok." Rachel looked down in an effort to both stop and hide the tears trying to form. Grace walked over to the table and put her arms around her. Rachel couldn't stop some of the tears from coming out, much as she tried.

"Ed has always been so good to me. Even in all this time since Derek and I broke up, he's always had a big hug and a smile for me."

"He's a good man. He's been working himself to de– *too hard*– lately. Shall we pray for them now before I call Evelyn?"

Rachel just nodded. *I miss being a part of that family. I should be with them now. Darn you, Derek. You ruined everything.*

Grace took Rachel's hand and began, "Heavenly Father, we know that You are in control of all things and we know that this did not slip by you unnoticed. We know that You love Ed and his family and we pray for Ed's healing and for the family's strength. Please let them feel Your presence and comfort while they sit at his bedside. Please use this situation for Your glory and their benefit."

She paused as if she were about to end the prayer, took a deep breath, and continued. "And Lord, please bring healing and peace to my dear, sweet Rachel. Please heal her heart and help her to forgive so she doesn't have to be captive to pain anymore. In Jesus' name we pray. Amen."

"Amen."

She kissed Rachel on the top of the head and walked into the kitchen to call Evelyn.

Rachel had lost her appetite and went upstairs to her room. She sat on her bed and stared at the wall. Memories of the

Cooper family flooded her as if a dam broke and there was nothing she could do to stop it.

She thought about Ed and the special connection she had always felt with him. He had been the one to take her to the dealership when she had finally saved up enough money to get a car, saying that everyone needed a dad with them for their first big purchase so they wouldn't get taken advantage of. He had been the one to help her with the insurance claims when someone rear-ended that car a year later. He had been the one to sit at the dining room table with Rachel and Derek as they filled out college applications and financial aid forms. He was also the one who teased her relentlessly and could always make her laugh. He was the closest thing Rachel had to a father in her life and she had looked forward to having him as her father-in-law.

Carol had played a huge part in Rachel's life, too. She had been a mother-figure and a mentor to her and helped fill the void left by her own mother. They had gone shopping and played games and gone for walks together when all the men in the family gathered around the TV for sports events and she was a great sounding board. She still sent handmade cards to Rachel for every holiday and special occasion and always let her know she was praying for her.

The Coopers were the only family she had ever felt a part of. Her grandmother was family, of course, but it was just the two of them. They were a *family*. They had accepted her as one of their own and now she couldn't be with them at a time when family should be together.

She was supposed to *be* a Cooper by now. If all had gone as planned, she and Derek would be celebrating their second wedding anniversary in February. *If all had gone as planned, I would be there comforting Ed and praying at his bedside right now. If only you'd been faithful and not blown it, I would be there comforting you* right now, Derek Cooper.

She needed to get lost in a book. She opened her laptop and started typing.

Chapter 8

Derek didn't know how much more he could take of staring silently at the screens in the hospital room. It was frustrating and exhausting sitting there unable to do anything. Ed was so heavily sedated that he was unaware of his family's presence or their prayers at his bedside.

Carol came in from talking with the nurses outside. "He's asleep and comfortable and the nurses said they would call us if anything changed. Let's take a walk to the cafeteria." *You read my mind.*

The three of them walked, and then sat, in silence.

Derek broke the ice. "How are you holding up, *really*, Mom?"

She broke into tears as she put her face in her hands. "I'm terrified. He's been under so much pressure for so long that this was bound to happen. *And I didn't do anything to stop it.*"

Clayton and Derek each put an arm around her. Clayton was the first to be able to form words. "This wasn't your fault, Mom. We've all seen the signs. We've all tried to help him in our own ways and he hasn't let us. He's going to be okay. He's strong and he'll fight this."

"He's only going to be okay if changes are made. I need help from both of you. I'm way too young to be a widow, and we're all going to need to be part of the change."

"Agreed." The brothers said in unison.

"If I had a 51% share in that miserable insurance agency, I would sell it today. It almost killed him and it would be good riddance."

Clayton and Derek shared a look and Derek spoke what they were both thinking. "If only it were that easy."

"You're right. Something needs to change, though, and I'm putting my foot down. Between now and the time your father gets out of this hospital, there will not be one word about work. The two of you will be handling everything there, and I don't want you to talk to him about any of it here. Agreed?"

"Yes, ma'am."

Carol walked up to the room and left her sons in charge of making a plan.

As much as he hated the circumstances, he was relieved that they were at the point where continuing as they had been was no longer an option.

"Clay, I'm so sick of that place. I want to help Dad – and you – but I don't know how to best do that. I was up all night looking at job postings. That's why I fell asleep in the chair and why my phone didn't get plugged in. When Mitch came over today, I was about to sit down and work on my resume. I was even ready to leave town. How's that for a bad son?" Derek looked down, feeling the guilt wash over him again.

"Do you think I haven't done that? Don't beat up on yourself. It's hard working there, and it's worse because neither of us chose our careers *or* the agency; Dad chose it for us. Remember a few years ago when I went through the same thing? I decided that I would make a go of it for a while and see what happened. And if it was still horrible, I was ready to go to Dad and quit. Remember that?"

"Yes. And you studied sales techniques and markets and got *really good* at sales."

"I did. I hate 98% of that business, but I love being in front of a customer, especially one who isn't really giving me the time of day. It's the thrill of the hunt, I guess. It reminds me of my days on the football field, except I don't have to worry about another torn ACL. If I'm honest, though, I'm not sure if I can go on like this long-term. That 98% is a heavy load."

"It is. Maybe I need to do what you did. Maybe I need to give myself a timeline and give it everything I've got and see what happens. Maybe I need to find my 2% that I can fall in love with and get good at. We know that our strengths don't overlap, so it would have to be an improvement for both of us. Now that Dad is in an Intensive Care Unit, I can't very well hand in my letter of resignation."

"Derek, we can do this. We've always held each other up, and now we need to hold Dad up, too. We need to find a way to step up, whether he likes it or not, so he can step back a bit. Maybe we would get *him* back."

"That would be great. I miss *having* a dad. Remember the old Thanksgiving days? We gave thanks and watched football and ate turkey and played cards and had a nice time together. Yesterday was awful. Now even holidays are like every other day. I can't even remember the last time we were together and we didn't talk about work. It's been out of control."

Clayton looked as sad as Derek felt. "All I could think about yesterday was how it seems like the business slowly sucked the life right out of Dad, and the family has followed."

Derek nodded. "That's all I could think about, too; that, and the fact that I saw Rachel with Ben Peterson on their way to Evelyn Glover's."

Clayton grimaced. "Oh, man. I'm sorry, brother. That explains your extra sour mood yesterday. What the heck is she doing with him?"

Derek clenched his jaw. "Apparently she likes boring now."

Chapter 9

Rachel jumped every time the phone rang. It was killing her not getting any updates. It had been almost 24 hours since they'd heard about Ed and no one had called to share how he was doing or if he was still in Intensive Care. Or if . . .

Grace walked into the living room. "A watched phone never rings, you know." She was gentle as she set a cup of tea in front of Rachel and patted her hand. Rachel's attempts to appear to be reading were apparently not fooling her.

"I know. I just want to know what's going on."

"I know you do." She gave her granddaughter a knowing look. "If things had taken a turn for the worst, we would have heard. Take that as good news."

"You're right. I hadn't thought of that. I just hate uncertainty."

"I know. You've had more than your share of uncertainty in your young life. Probably more than most people have in an entire lifetime." Rachel's eyes clouded over as Grace continued. "You know, even when you were a little girl, you hated not knowing what was going on. Growing up with a mother who was sick and couldn't take care of herself, let alone you, you learned to be the adult at an age when you shouldn't have had a care in the world. I think that's why you're so responsible and independent. But I also think that's why sometimes you think you should be able to make every situation better, that there should be something you can do. You can't turn back time and take away Ed's heart attack, but maybe there's something you can do to show your support for him."

"I want to go visit him so badly. I want to be able to see him for myself and just sit with him and Carol. But I don't want to run into Derek. I know I should be over how emotional I get when I see him, but I'm not."

"I know. When you love someone that much, they never really leave your heart. You'll deal with that when you're ready. But in the meantime, Derek has a business to run while Ed is recovering, so he's not going to be at the hospital 24 hours a day."

The next day, Ed Cooper was the talk of the church. He was well-known and well-loved in the community and everyone committed to praying for him and helping with food and chores as he recovered. Rachel was worn out from praying and remembering and wondering what to do.

Pastor Ray talked about the uncertainty of life and not knowing what tomorrow brings. He encouraged the parishioners to tell the people around them how they felt about them, to offer apologies and forgiveness as often as necessary, and to keep short accounts. He also stressed the importance of keeping short accounts with God; confess what needs to be confessed, accept forgiveness that's offered, and go on about doing His work.

Rachel felt convicted that she needed to offer more forgiveness to Derek, to her mother, and to her unknown father, whether forgiveness was asked for or not. *Lord, please help me with this. I know that I hold on to the anger and use it to protect myself, but I also know that it doesn't work. I know I can forgive my mother because I know she loves me and tries and that she has challenges that I don't understand. I know I can forgive my father because I don't even know him; he's no more than an idea. The hardest one is Derek. He knew me and supposedly loved me and chose to betray me. He was the one I loved and trusted and felt safe with. He's the one I thought would never hurt me. It's terrifying to ask You to take the anger away because all I'll be left with is the hurt, but the anger is like a weight that's pulling me down and I don't even feel like myself anymore. Please help me with this and bring me back to the person I was before the hurt got to be too much. Please heal the hurt and take the anger and help me to forgive.*

As she and Ben cleaned up the kitchen during the fellowship time at church, he acted as if he had something he wanted to say. That always made Rachel tense up a bit.

"Pastor Ray really made me think today when he talked about needing to have more conversations with the people in our lives so there are no misunderstandings or anything unspoken. That goes for both the tough *and* encouraging things in my book. When we were at Evelyn's on Thanksgiving, I was thinking about the things I'm thankful for. One of the things I'm thankful for is our friendship." He seemed a bit nervous and Rachel braced herself for what was coming next.

Drat! No, no, no! She tried to plaster what she hoped was a pleasant but non-encouraging expression on her face and waited for him to spit it out.

He continued. "It's really nice to have a friend to spend time with. I'm glad we got to know each other through the book club and that we get to share the things we have in common. And I'm glad that you're not any more interested in dating than I am." He gave her a half smile.

She exhaled and tried not to let out a whoop. *Whew! Add perceptive to Ben's list of attributes.*

She smiled back at him, filled with relief. "You know that half the town thinks we're a couple, right?"

He laughed. "It's ok with me if it's okay with you. It keeps the older ladies around here from trying to fix me up."

"Me too."

Chapter 10

Derek was worn out. He and Clayton had been taking turns at the hospital all week, switching at lunch time, so each was able to be both at the hospital and at the office every day. Since Dad had been having a lot of side effects from the medications they were filling him with, his hospital stay was stretching into its second week.

He was in a regular room on the cardiac unit, which was much better than Intensive Care, and a cot had been brought in for Carol. Derek and Clayton had both offered, and even begged, to stay with him so she could sleep in her own bed, but she wouldn't hear of it. She wasn't leaving his side for a second. *She probably wants to make sure he doesn't try to do any work.*

He poured some coffee to help him stay awake for the drive and headed for his car. Usually he took the morning shift at the hospital, but Clayton had some meetings that he couldn't move to the morning at the office, so today Derek was going for the afternoon shift.

As tired as he had been all week, now that he was crawling out of his funk a bit, he had enjoyed the sunrise coming over the hills every morning as he made the drive. He wasn't fully himself yet, or he would have been letting out the "oohs" and "ahhs" that normally escaped his lips every time he came over a hill or a curve and got a fresh view of God's palette of colors. Still, the combination of fall color and the morning sun was once again breathtaking.

The ladies at church had arranged for people to bring over some snacks and foods that would transport easily and that they could keep in the hospital room for them, so Derek had a cooler packed. He looked over at the old cooler and thought of the times that he and Rachel had filled it with junk food and hauled it around Summit County for day-long picnics.

They had picnics in every type of setting, from the beaches to the slopes of Summit Mountain to the woods. When it was too cold to actually *be* outside, they moved the picnics to their living rooms and to his car, parking it at the beach or on the bluffs overlooking Lake Michigan. He usually had his camera with him to capture scenes he wanted to paint. They even had picnics in each others' dorm rooms and apartments when they visited each other at their respective colleges. Their roommates thought they were weird, but that just made them more fun. Picnics were their special thing.

He was too tired to fight the memories as he drove over the rolling hills, so he let them play in his mind like a documentary. Images of skiing, hiking in the woods, playing games, laughing over inside jokes, driving along Lake Michigan, studying together, walking out to the lighthouse . . . the images both warmed and broke his heart.

He wished he could crawl back into the memories. He eventually came to the part in his internal movie where she suddenly stopped talking to him. He remembered that part way too vividly and felt his chest tighten.

It was the end of spring semester of their junior year in college. He had been working on a portrait of her for weeks. Since he wanted it to be a surprise, and she never would have posed for it anyway, he had traded modeling time with a girl in one of his art classes. She was working on a graphic novel and needed someone to pose as her main character. She was a great model for his project because her build and hair were similar to Rachel's.

He wanted the portrait to be perfect and spent more time on it than any project he'd ever done. He had long before memorized every angle of Rachel's face, so that was the easy part. The hard part was showing the real Rachel in it, making the portrait come alive.

When the girl whose name he didn't even remember had agreed to pose, he knew he could create the portrait he dreamed of creating. Between the two projects, they had spent so much time together in that art room that they had to squelch rumors that there was more than drawing going on.

After weeks of working on it, he was finally satisfied with the finished product. He had taken it to the frame shop off campus and had taken an hour to wrap it in a way that would look as special as the contents.

He drove the hour and fifteen minutes to her school feeling like a kid who had just taken down a giant with a slingshot. He saw her car in the parking lot of her apartment, but she didn't answer the door. He called and texted, but got no answer. He finally texted her roommate after sitting in the parking lot and not hearing anything back for two hours, and she told him Rachel had nothing to say to him.

From that point forward, she wouldn't talk to or even look at him. She refused to tell him what he had done, saying only, "you know." He *didn't* know. He had racked his brain trying to figure out what he possibly could have done and came up with nothing. He had tried sending letters and flowers but she had returned them.

After weeks of trying, he came to the conclusion that the only way he could show her he loved her was to give her the time and space she wanted. Never in his wildest dreams did he think that three and a half years later she would be out of his life.

Eventually he had tried dating and had met some nice girls, but none of them made his heart skip a beat. None of them stimulated his mind. None of them got his jokes. None of them shared his heart for God. None of them were Rachel.

It had been three and a half years since he'd been able to look into her beautiful honey brown eyes. Three and a half years since he'd been able to hold her in his arms. Three and a half years since he'd felt like *himself*. He'd felt as though he'd been living in some type of dark parallel universe ever since.

He forced the images out of his mind and prayed for his father.

He arrived at the hospital shortly after one. He had found a side entrance with better parking and felt like an old pro navigating the back way to his father's room. As he came around the corner, he looked right into those beautiful brown eyes that he had missed so much. *Rachel.*

Chapter 11

Rachel came around the corner and froze. *What the—*

"Rachel!"

"Derek!" *No! He's supposed to come in the mornings!* When she saw how tired and worried he looked, it took everything in her not to hug him. Out of reflex she grabbed her anger instead.

He looked like he had to scramble for words. "What are you doing here?"

I'm a grown woman who doesn't need to explain herself to lying, cheating cheaters. That's what I'm doing here.

She felt the sting of conviction as she was reminded of her grandmother's prayer and Pastor Ray's sermon about forgiveness and her own prayers for the ability to forgive, and held back her sarcasm.

"I came to see your mom and dad." She wished she could run down the hall, out of his gravitational pull.

"Oh, uh, great! I'm sure they'll be thrilled to see you. His room is this way." He started to gesture down the hall and she knew she needed to be honest.

"I know where his room is. This– This isn't the first time I've visited. I've just planned it for–"

"For when I wasn't here." His face fell and he looked hurt as he was probably figuring out that his family had kept her visits a secret from him. Even though he had crushed her, she didn't want to hurt him back. She kicked herself for feeling sorry for him.

"I figured it would be easier for both of us." She looked down to avoid the pain she saw on his face. "I'm sorry; I didn't mean to cause any friction. I just wanted to see your dad. Have a nice visit."

Now I feel like a fool. Why did I think this was a good idea?

She didn't want him to see the tears that were threatening to form, so she turned quickly and half-walked, half-ran for the elevator, punching the *Door Close* button as soon as she stepped in, then several more times in case the signal didn't get through.

She tried to call Brianna and Shelby when she got into her car, but only got their voice mails.

"Okay, Lord, I guess I have to talk to You about this. I mean, I want to talk to You, but– You know what I mean. It's probably good that they didn't answer because You're the One I *should* be talking to.

"You know I've been praying about forgiving him, and I'm trying, I really am. But why did I have to *see* him?" She gripped the steering wheel and fought her tears. She hated tears and always fought them.

"I'm sorry, Lord. I can't even talk to You about this right now. I promise we'll talk when I get home, ok?"

She drove in silence for the next few minutes, and then the words came flooding out in a torrent. "Why, Lord, *why*? Why did he have to change his schedule today? Why did we have to come from opposite directions and almost collide? Why did he have to have our old *picnic cooler* in his hands? Is he having a picnic in the hospital room? Or maybe he packed a picnic to impress a nurse!"

She immediately felt bad. It was obvious that he had barely slept since this started over a week ago. The worry on his face and grey tinge in his normally blue eyes was about more than seeing her.

"I'm sorry, Lord. I know I should be praying for him, not accusing him of bad behavior. Please be with him and give him the comfort that only You can give. Please take care of him physically and give him a good night of sleep tonight. Please give him the peace that passes all understanding and remind him that you work all things together for good. And please help me to fully forgive him."

For the first time in three and a half years, she had compassion for Derek Cooper. And it terrified her.

Chapter 12

Derek's head was spinning as he walked to his father's room. *Rachel. Rachel has been coming here.*

He was angry and hurt at his family for keeping it from him, but quickly realized that they did it to protect him. *And maybe themselves.* As sullen as he had been lately, no one would have wanted to draw the short straw and be tasked with being the messenger with that news.

You can't blame them for not wanting to deal with your wrath. Forget about it and be a nice visitor.

Ed was up in a chair and smiled when Derek walked into the room. His mother looked exhausted, but she was beaming.

"The doctor says our patient is doing well enough that we can talk about discharge."

Derek patted his father's arm, careful to avoid the IV line. "That's great news, Dad. You're both going to feel much better after sleeping in your own bed."

"Is there any food in that cooler for me? The heart attack didn't kill me, but today's slop from the cafeteria might." It was good to see that Dad's sense of humor had returned. It had been way too long since he'd seen that side of him.

Derek opened the cooler and put on his best waiter impression to display the food he'd brought. Ed deferred to Carol to choose first. *Always the gentleman. These are the qualities I want to think of when I think of you, Dad. Not anger and frustration and control.*

They chatted about the goings on in Hideaway and the preparations the town was making for Christmas. They chatted about the hospital staff and the terrible food from the cafeteria. They chatted about the upcoming Advent activities at church. They chatted about everything except work.

Carol had shared her moratorium on that topic with Ed, and apart from a few slip ups, he had obeyed. It was glorious. Derek was starting to think that Ed was enjoying the break from his work responsibilities and the obsession that they had fueled.

Carol excused herself to go down the hall for a walk and some coffee, and Ed turned to Derek. "Son, we need to talk about the agency."

Derek's heart sank. *No. This has been so nice.*

"This has been a real wake-up call for me, and your mother has made it abundantly clear that she is not planning to join the widow's group at church any time soon or stay with the status quo. Since I've been in this place, I've had a lot of conversations with her and with God about my life and my future. I don't know what things will look like, but I've promised them both that things will change. And I'm promising you that things will change, too. I promise, son." He looked him square in the eye.

47

Father and son both welled up with tears. "We're going to have a family discussion and make decisions *together* when I get out of here."

"Should we have EMS on standby during that discussion?" Derek grinned sarcastically at his dad.

Ed laughed. "That's not a bad idea, but it won't be necessary. I'm a changed man. Well, at least a *changing* man. You know I take my promises seriously."

Derek's smile was full of relief. "I know you do."

He leaned over and hugged his dad. "It's so good to have you back, Dad. I've missed you."

Chapter 13

Rachel flopped on her bed and stared at the ceiling. *What a day*.

She couldn't get the image of Derek out of her head. He looked so tired, so afraid, so *defeated*. She had never seen him look like that before.

She couldn't imagine what he was going through, what it must be like for him to have to think about losing his father. Ed wasn't just his father, either. He was his hero, the one he aspired to be. At least that was how it used to be.

She wondered what that would be like, to admire a parent enough to want to be like them. She had never known her father or anything about him, and she felt sorry for her mother. Emergencies with her mother involved finding a new doctor who would prescribe narcotics after another one stopped trying or trying a new rehab or finding a place to live after moving out of a boyfriend's home, not Intensive Care Units. Rachel didn't even know where she was living half the time and hadn't heard from her in a few months. Her upbringing and family life could not have been more different from Derek's.

His family life was one of the things Rachel missed most about being with him. She thought back to high school and the family game nights they had included her in. Clayton was off at college, so it was an easy fit to have her fill his chair for Euchre or any other game they chose.

The laughter and easy conversation around their dining room table filled her with joy. It had forever been cemented in her mind as the definition of family time.

She and Derek were juniors in high school when he finally told her that he had been harboring the same secret feelings for her that she had for him and they made the leap from best buddies and study partners to joined-at-the-hip lovebirds. They realized early on in their relationship that if they were going to keep their purity promises to God and to each other, they would need to spend a lot of time either with others in the room or doing things together in public. They delighted in playing footsies under the table during family game nights and loved the idea that they were getting away with something right under his parents' noses. Working together at River's Edge Canoes in the summer and at Summit Mountain in the winter gave them a perfect balance between spending time together and having people and tasks to keep them on the straight and narrow. Still, they were known to steal kisses on breaks as often as possible.

"What happened, Lord? How did everything go so wrong? I thought he loved me as much as I loved him. We had agreed *together* that we were going to wait for our wedding night, and I thought he was as committed as I was. Why did he throw it all away for some other girl? Why wasn't what we had enough for him? *Why wasn't I enough for him?*"

She hit the nerve that she always hit when she tried to pray or talk about Derek. She wasn't enough for him, just like she wasn't enough for her mother to stay with treatment and she wasn't enough for her father to acknowledge her existence.

"Lord, help me to fully forgive them. It doesn't matter that they haven't begged for my forgiveness. Well, Mom has. You know what I mean, Lord. Forgiving isn't about them, it's about me. They can't repay what they took, but I can forgive them and release all of us." She took in a deep breath.

"I forgive Mom for being weak. I forgive my father for not caring enough to show up. I forgive Derek for turning to another girl. I forgive them. Help me to do this."

She wiped her eyes, blew her nose, and pulled out her laptop. *Creating people is much easier than dealing with them in real life.*

She had started writing historical fiction after she broke up with Derek. After getting her heart crushed, it was a great escape for her. Over the years, she had written dozens of short books.

She started with mystery books and found them pretty easy to write, then expanded to light romance. She had published most of the shorter books under a pseudonym without mentioning a word to anyone. It was a nice supplement to her income and the reviews gave her confidence in her writing and joy that others enjoyed the history in them as much as she did. It wasn't that she was ashamed of her writing, but she felt that it wasn't *hers*, so she didn't see the point in sharing it. The historical context in the stories was her research, but the writing style was one she adopted from other writers in the genre, especially Kristin Hamilton, her favorite. The writing came easy, but it didn't come naturally. She just wrote the books she thought others would enjoy.

Her true love when it came to writing was historical fiction that explored deep questions of the human condition and events that gripped her heart. She had written two full novels, one about a family that helped the Underground Railroad and one about a man who struggled with whether or not to support and join the American Revolution. Because the introspective literary novels were written in her own voice, no one would have guessed that they were written by the same person who wrote the light genre books.

She figured that since she had no plans to actually publish them, even under a pseudonym, she could completely be herself and write the way she wanted to write. The writing flowed from deep within her and the pleasure she derived was from the writing, not from any thought of having another soul read them.

Chapter 14

Derek and Clayton rode together to the hospital to pick up their parents. It was the first time they had been with each other for more than a passing moment since they'd been splitting time between the hospital and the office.

Clayton typed away on his laptop while Derek drove.

"What are you working on?"

"Hold up . . . just . . . one . . . second." He held up his finger, then saved the document and put the device in his bag.

"Ok, I've been working on some ideas that have come out of the things you and I have always talked about, and wanted to have all of them in my notes before I talked to you and Dad about them. I didn't want to take the chance of forgetting anything important." Derek admired Clayton's perseverance and desire to make the family's business situation work.

"Ideas? What kind of ideas?" Derek could see Clayton's excitement, and didn't want to see him get his hopes dashed again. "Do you think Dad will really listen?"

"I think he has to. He could have died and that's a wake-up call you can't ignore. He told both of us he wants to make decisions together and he looked sincere to me. I think he's been relieved to be away from the office, even if it's been because he was in a hospital. He seems ready for change."

"Let's hope. You and I have been ready for change for a long time and he's been the one resisting."

"At the risk of sounding morbid, I was thinking we could start the conversation while we're waiting for the discharge paperwork to come through. That way, if he gets upset and tries to have another heart attack, there will be people there to help. I cleared it with Mom, too."

"You were always the idea man when it came to handling Dad, Clayton. I don't care of it *is* morbid. It sounds *safe*." He glanced at his brother. "Care to share the ideas with me now?"

The plan to start the conversation in the hospital room was brilliant. No one would yell with all those witnesses, and if anyone needed medical attention, it was there.

"Dad, Derek and I have been talking about some ideas for how to go forward with the agency."

Ed looked curious. "Go on."

Wait, what just happened? Did Dad just indicate that he's open to listening? He has changed.

"We've both been working full time at the agency since we've been out of college, so I've had almost six years to learn and observe and Derek has had almost three. We've also seen what our friends are doing to adapt to the way business is done, and we've gotten a chance to see what's worked for them and what hasn't."

"And you have some ideas?"

Derek and Clayton shared a look.

Clayton continued, "Well, we've always had ideas, but they didn't fit what you wanted to do with your agency."

Derek was impressed by the lack of bitterness in Clayton's voice and the gentle look on his face. *No wonder he's so good at sales.*

"Frankly, that was our fault. We came in as hot shots with college degrees and thought we knew everything. No wonder you didn't listen to us. You were right not to listen when we were fresh out of school and full of arrogance. But you've told us throughout our lives that you wanted us to take over the agency. If it's going to become *our* agency, as in the three – four – of us," he gestured to include his mother, "then we will all need to have a say in the direction . . . *and* in the operation."

"You're right. You *were* arrogant." Ed winked at them. "But so was I. Even though your youthful arrogance is gone, I stopped listening so long ago that I didn't realize it. All I wanted to do was have a successful business to pass on to you, but I lost the plot somewhere in the last few years. I was so afraid of losing the business that I lost sight of *why* I wanted it to be successful in the first place. I wanted to pass it on to you boys. I can't pass it on while keeping a white-knuckle grip on it."

Derek sat stunned. "Dad, Clay is speaking for both of us, but I want you to hear directly from me too that I'm sorry. I was arrogant and I didn't listen to you either. You built that business because you were good at it and I just took it as fact that Clay and I had better answers than you because they were new. Saying it makes me realize how stupid it sounds." He looked at his parents sheepishly. "I'm sorry."

Ed smiled at Carol. "Look, honey! Our boys are learning." The family shared a laugh for the first time in a long time.

"Ok, let me have it while I still have this call button to the nurses station. What are your ideas?"

Chapter 15

Rachel, Shelby, and Brianna had started exchanging Christmas presents on the first Saturday of December when they were in 9th grade. They did it so that if they bought clothes for each other, they could have something new to wear to Christmas parties.

They had slumber parties at Rachel's the night before, opened their presents in their pajamas, and pretended it was Christmas Day. Grandma even made her special Christmas sausage casserole and coffee cake and wished them Merry Christmas throughout the day.

Even though they had moved on to different kinds of gifts over the years, the tradition, including the slumber party and gift opening in pajamas, remained intact. In recent years they had moved it to over Thanksgiving break, but since Rachel was the only one in town this year, she'd suggested they just exchange gifts when they were all together for Christmas. Brianna and Shelby vetoed her idea immediately, invoking unbreakable tradition and moving it back to the original date in early December.

They had all received their packages in the mail and had planned for a conference call so they could open them 'together' in pajamas over morning coffee.

Rachel was excited for them to open their gifts. She had gotten matching bracelets for all of them that had all of their birthstones on them, and gotten them each a book, of course. Brianna's was easy. *The MBA's Guide to the Real World* would come in handy in a few months when she received hers. Shelby's, on the other hand, took months of research because Rachel wanted to find something that would be useful and that she wouldn't already have. Shelby had been fighting chronic illness for the past five years, which was why instead of a master's degree, she was about to graduate with her bachelor's. *Healing Herbs: Recipes for Living* won the competition based on Rachel's research, and because the classic was old and out of print, there was a good chance she wouldn't already have it.

Rachel had just one package to open, as the others had gone in on her gift. They got uncharacteristically quiet as she opened it. It was a subscription to a genealogy website with a DNA test kit included. Rachel stared at the package containing the cotton swab.

Rachel had had an interest in genealogy since she was a teenager. Her grandmother had always had the same interest, so she had volumes of information on her side of the family, which had been traced back to the Mayflower. Rachel had subscribed to websites whenever they had free trials to see if she could find out more and she and her grandmother celebrated every time they learned something new.

Her family tree was one-sided, though. She didn't even know her father's name or what his relationship with her mother had been like, let alone any of his family history. She didn't even know if he was dead or alive.

"Is it ok that we did that, Rachel? Maybe this will give you some answers." Shelby's voice dripped with concern.

"Wow, you guys. I'm just taken aback. Even combining for the gift, you went over our budget."

"We thought this was important enough to break the budget. Since it's a gift, the membership doesn't start until you submit the swab. You need this, Rachel. You need answers. Even though your mom has never told you anything about him, you can still find out about where that side of your family came from. It's *something* and maybe it will help." Brianna was gentle but firm.

"You're right; I do need this. Any information would be more than what I have now Thank you, you guys. I mean it."

"We'll even hold off until we come home for Christmas to start nagging you about sending the swab in, ok?"

"Well, *you* might, Shelby. *I* want her to send it in now so that we can be there when the results come in!"

"Wait, is *this* why we couldn't wait to open the gifts when we're all together?"

Brianna laughed. "You're welcome."

The call went on for an hour after they opened their gifts. Rachel told them about almost literally running into Derek at the hospital the day before. Both of them saw it as divine intervention and said that the time had come for them to have a conversation.

Brianna was blunt, as always. "You two have both been miserable for three and a half years. I miss the real you. It's long past time for the two of you to sit down and talk so that you can tell him all the ways he hurt you and he can say whatever it is he has to say. He needs to fess up and apologize and you need to forgive him. At that point, you can either make up and live happily ever after together or walk away from each other with a clean slate to start fresh with someone else. Neither of those things can happen if you avoid him forever."

"You know she's right. We want you to be you again and see you really *live*, instead of just existing and hanging out with Boring Ben."

Brianna, true to form, asked, "So, are you going to send the DNA swab first, or talk to Derek first?"

Chapter 16

The Cooper family had been sitting at the dining room table for four hours. They had gone to church and lunch after, then came home and got down to business. The table was covered with reports, spreadsheets, and note pads. Carol had taken on the role of facilitator and together they had come up with what they saw as the strengths and weaknesses of the agency and of each other.

They had agreed that their goal was health and family unity first and successful business second. They had prayed as a family as well, asking God for guidance, wisdom, and courage to make tough decisions, and asking Him to help them to listen to Him and each other. There had not been one raised voice.

Carol was a great facilitator. She was using her skills honed over 32 years as a teacher to manage the dining room full of men who had the potential to act like unruly children, and she was getting results. She even brought out her white board.

They found that they agreed on most of the strengths and weaknesses of the business itself, which helped them to take a hard look at themselves to see where their own strengths and weaknesses could help the agency and each other. They realized quickly that much of the conflict they'd had was because there were no defined roles, and discussed ways to reduce the overlap and coordinate better with each other.

Derek would be the primary person reviewing the policies, using his strength with details. He would also take on some of the marketing so he could exercise his creativity. Clayton would keep his primary focus on sales and work on ways to weave technology into customer service, and Ed would stay at the helm guiding the agency on its mission and networking.

Derek felt like he was in a dream. "Do you realize this is the first time we've ever looked at the business as a family and looked at it as a tool for the family to use instead of as its master?"

"And all it took was the threat of death." Ed laughed at his own joke, then paused and turned serious. "I feel like Abraham sitting here. God threatened death to save my life and test my heart. From here on out, the business serves the family, not the other way around." *There's my wise dad. It's so good to have him back.*

"We need a break from this topic and this table. Let's go out for dinner." Carol even facilitated dinner flawlessly.

"But honey, we've got all those casseroles in the fridge."

They all laughed and raced each other to the front door. "It's too bad Bellows Vineyards is closed for the season. I feel like celebrating. How about the Birchwood Inn?"

Chapter 17

Rachel wondered what was going on with Ben. They had just had the conversation cementing just-friends status a week before, and now he had asked her out to dinner. They'd never gone out to dinner other than after working on a project at the library, and certainly had never gone to someplace as nice as the Birchwood Inn.

He had said he had news for her and that he wanted to thank her. She wasn't sure what his news could be and couldn't imagine what he could possibly need to thank her for, other than providing cover from well-meaning ladies who wanted to fix him up with their nieces.

The Birchwood Inn was busy for this time of year, but they were able to be seated quickly. It was a small place, even by Summit County standards. The cherry wood walls were the perfect background for the paintings of birch trees and the sculptures made out of birch branches. All the wood and candles made it seem especially cozy on a cold evening.

She carefully avoided looking at the painting the owners had commissioned from Derek after high school that hung proudly over the stone fireplace. She also carefully avoided remembering being with him when he took the pictures of the birch tree on the Empire Bluff Trail or choosing which one to use for it.

While they waited for their food, Rachel noticed that Ben was more animated than she had ever seen him. Considering the fact that she'd rarely seen him animated, that wasn't much of a stretch, but still.

"Rachel, I want to let you in on something. I've been writing some poetry and I'm thinking about publishing it." He said it as if that's just what people did. They wrote things and published them under their own names. Instead of writing them in secret and hiding them in boxes in closets or publishing them under aliases without telling even their best friends, they published them and told people.

Once she got over her shock at the thought of sharing one's work with the world, she was overcome by excitement for Ben.

"Good for you, Ben! That's so exciting!" She held up her hot cocoa for a toast. Just as they were clinking their mugs, she saw the Cooper family enter the restaurant out of the corner of her eye.

Oh, great. Derek, twice in one week. What are You doing to me, Lord? She willed her eyes to stay on Ben and acted as if she hadn't seen them.

Fortunately Ben didn't seem to notice and continued. "I wanted to celebrate with you and thank you, because our talks about books inspired me to share what I've been working on. You're the only one I trust to share it with right now." The phrase 'trust to share' stung a bit.

"Wow, I'm honored."

"Are you honored enough to read it and be my editor?"

Chapter 18

Of all the restaurants in all the towns in all of Summit County, she walks into this one. The Humphrey Bogart impression in his head was spot on.

They were looking mighty cozy over there, clinking coffee mugs and smiling at each other. He had quickly glanced down to make sure there was no ring on her left hand as he walked to his table. He was relieved to see that wasn't the reason for the big smiles.

Thank God that the family and work situations are improving, because that little scene might have put me right over the edge.

His mom squeezed his arm and gave him a knowing look. She had told him about Rachel's visits to the hospital and he had told her about their surprise meeting in the hallway. He had quickly accepted her apology for keeping the visits from him, telling her he would have done the same thing in her situation. It was comforting talking to her about Rachel for the first time in a long time, and her compassion for him was healing.

Fortunately, the table they were shown to was on the other end of the small room, near the fireplace. He chose the chair that faced away from the scene still playing in his head and making his heart feel heavy.

Lord? May I please have a break? He said it in his nicest, most polite internal voice.

He resolved to focus on his family, now that they were trying out their newly minted rule of no business talk at meals. Somehow the topic of their elementary and middle school art projects came up and set off a flurry of stories. He had never been so happy to talk about paper mache, dioramas, and pottery bowls in his life.

"I still love to see your birch painting here, Derek. I haven't seen any new art at your house in ages, or anywhere for that matter. Have I been so busy that I've missed it, or have I kept you so busy that you haven't had time?" Ed's question turned all eyes to Derek.

"I've been too busy to even think about it." *And haven't been able to pick up a paint brush or even a pencil since I finished a certain portrait a while back.*

"Well, I hope now that we're streamlining things, you'll have more time. You've got a special talent and I miss seeing your work." Derek tried to hide his surprise. *You miss my work? I thought you only tolerated my art once I graduated from high school.*

Ed continued, "You know, I've been told I need to take up a hobby to 'manage my stress' a few hundred times lately. What do you think? Do you think I should try it? Maybe you got your talent from my side of the family." He winked at his wife and she groaned.

Clayton knew Derek's discomfort with the topic of his art these days and spoke up. "I would love to see you go back to your woodworking, Dad. Remember the stuff you used to make for us when we were younger? I still have some of those toys in my old closet so I can pass them on to my kids." *Clayton saves the day again.* He was the only one who knew how long it had been since Derek had created anything and why his creativity had dried up. His comment sent off a flurry of stories about the toys and games Dad had made for them and the spotlight left Derek.

He gave his brother a slight nod of thanks and looked over at his mother. She looked so peaceful and contented, like a woman who had her family back.

Chapter 19

Rachel put down Ben's manuscript pages and rubbed her eyes. She hated reading on screens and was glad he had taken the time to print out the pages instead of sending her a file. She wondered if some of her writing would look any different to her if it was printed out on a fresh page without markings and coffee stains all over it.

Ben had inspired her. His writing was quite good, but it wasn't the writing that was the source of her inspiration this morning. He had a dream and *tried* something. He put his work out there. That took bravery.

As someone who had come to live her life in self-protective mode, that was a foreign concept. She decided that she was going to be brave, too. She walked over to her desk, pulled out the envelope with the DNA swab in it and opened the sterile package.

"Here we go, Lord. If You have any answers You want to give me through this, please do. I know this can only tell me so much, but I'd like to know a little bit about my father's family and heritage. Actually, I'd like to know as much as You want to tell me."

She rubbed the swab on the inside of her cheek and put it into the return package quickly so that she didn't have time to change her mind. She drove to the post office and took a video of her hand dropping it into the mail box. She felt very brave as she shared the video into the group text with Brianna and Shelby.

As she was walking out, Derek was coming up the walk with his arms full of packages to be sent. *Seriously, Lord? Okay, fine. I'll take this as Your cue.*

She took a deep breath and looked directly at him. It was time for her next brave act for the day.

Chapter 20

"**R**achel. Hi." *Probably came to the post office to deliver a late afternoon kiss to her boyfriend. Things may be better in my life, but I'm still not crazy about small towns.*

"Hi." She looked down at her feet but stood still. He wasn't sure what to make of the fact that she wasn't running away.

"Is everything ok?"

She looked even more nervous than she usually did around him these days as she spoke. "Yes. No. Yes. Umm, how's your dad?"

"He's getting stronger every day. He's grateful to be alive and to have a fresh start." *What I wouldn't give for a fresh start of my own.* She just nodded, looking at the ground behind him.

"You should go see him sometime now that he's at home. They told me how much they enjoyed your visits at the hospital and I know they would both love to see you." He paused. "I'll make sure not to go over there then so you can be comfortable. Just let me know when and I'll stay away. I'm sorry I messed up your visit that day at the hospital." The boxes he was carrying felt like they weighed two hundred pounds. His legs felt even heavier. He reminded himself to breathe.

"Ok, I'll do that. Thanks." She hesitated, as if she was willing herself to continue. "Um, Derek, could we talk sometime? I know it's way overdue, but I have some things to say and I imagine you do, too."

Bombs exploded in his head.

"Sure, of course. Where?"

She looked surprised. "I hadn't thought that far ahead. I'd like for us to have some privacy. Would you mind coming to my house? Or I could go to yours. I just don't want to be in public for such a private conversation."

His legs got even heavier. *Are we finally going to have the conversation? Am I finally going to have a chance to find out what I did wrong? Or maybe she's going to tell me she's engaged. Well, I might as well get it over with.*

"We could go to your house right now, if you'd like. Or mine. I just need to get these packages dropped off for my mom."

"Okay." She stood for a moment, thinking. "My grandma is at Evelyn's for Bridge Club this afternoon, so my house is free. I just have to make a quick stop on the way home. Can you meet me there in half an hour?"

More explosions in his head. *Are you kidding me?* "I'll be there."

He texted Clayton as soon as he put down the packages to tell him he wouldn't be returning to the office and why and asked him to pray.

Chapter 21

By the time Rachel pulled into her driveway, the knot in her stomach had engulfed her entire body. She took one last breath and closed her eyes.

"Ok, Lord. Show me how to do this. Grandma and Shelby and Brianna are right. I've forgiven him, but I need healing. Maybe if I get some answers, I can move on from this."

She looked at the thick brown envelope on the seat next to her and picked it up carefully. "If I'm brave enough to send my DNA through the mail and print a fresh draft of one of my real manuscripts, I'm brave enough to say what I need to say and put this relationship to rest." She sent a quick urgent prayer request to the group text with Shelby and Brianna and forced herself out of the car.

She convinced herself that her nerves were only about having a difficult conversation, that they had nothing to do with being in a room with Derek with no distractions. She tried not to think about his blue eyes and the little bit of late afternoon dirty blonde stubble starting on his jaw. She tried to focus on what she wanted to say and how she wanted to say it.

He arrived right on time. He stood on the porch with his hands in his pockets looking like he was trying to fit his elbows in too. It was obvious that he was as nervous as she was. His eyes looked grey, as they always did when he was worried.

She offered him some tea that she'd had just enough time to make and he accepted. She thought of bringing a gallon of water along too, to combat the drought that had just started in her mouth.

He sat on the end of the couch and it looked like he was taking in the room. It had been almost four years since he had been in this room and he was probably noting the changes. The warm brown paint was a great step up from the worn wallpaper that used to be there, and the refinished coffee table looked new. She wondered if he was thinking about how much more comfortable the couch he was sitting on was than its predecessor. He used to say that when he graduated from college and got his first paycheck, his first purchase was going to be a softer couch for Grandma.

She realized he was looking at her, waiting for her to say something.

"Um, thank you for coming. I'm not really sure where to start, but I thought that it would be a good idea for us to finally talk about what happened between us. Well, I think it would be a good idea for me to, at least. I hope that's ok with you." *I should have taken more time to practice what to say in the car.*

What looked like relief flashed across his face and his eyes were gentle and expectant. "I've been waiting for three and a half years to have this conversation, Rachel, so yes, it's ok with me. Take your time."

"Ok. Well, uh, I need to know why you did what you did. No. Wait. I need to start with telling you that I know I wasn't the best girlfriend or fiancée or whatever you want to call what I was. I know I got upset easily and shut down and didn't know how to handle things well when we argued or I felt insecure. I'm very sorry about that." She forced herself to look intently into his eyes. "What I really need to know is why you cheated on me."

His eyes grew wide. "Why I *what*? You thought I *cheated* on you?"

"Derek, come on. It's been a long time now. It took me a long time, but I've forgiven you. I just want to know why so I can understand." *Maybe if I understand, I can forget about you.* She tried to hide the tears forming in her eyes.

His voice was full of hurt. "Where on earth did you get that idea? Rachel, please look at me. *Please.*"

She summoned all her strength and looked at him through tears. His eyes were as full as hers.

"Rach, I never cheated on you. I never looked at another girl or thought of another girl. You were my *everything*." His voice was barely a whisper and it took him a minute to continue. "Why did you think that I *cheated* on you?"

Rachel's heart sank. She wished she could crawl through the floor boards. He looked like he was telling the truth. He looked *crushed*. She reminded herself that looks could be deceiving, though, and she forced herself to continue.

"Molly – my roommate – was down at State visiting a friend and she said she saw you with another girl in the dorm. She asked her friend about it and her friend said you two were always together. She said the girl had a reputation for having overnight male visitors and she was sure you had been one. Molly said she even looked like me from far away."

That's the worst part. I wasn't enough to wait for, but someone who looked like me was enough to throw away everything we had over. It made her sick to even tell the story. She swallowed a sip of tea to keep her lunch down.

Recognition crossed his face and it was obvious he knew exactly who she was talking about. He put his head in his hands as she gripped the arms of her chair, bracing herself for the confession.

He raised his head and looked her in the eye. "I know who you're talking about. She was a girl in my art class. We took turns modeling for each other. I was the model for a graphic novel she was writing and she was the model for a portrait I was painting . . . of *you*." He sounded like he was choking on his words.

He looked at her through his tears and it felt like his eyes were burning into her. "I swear to you, Rachel. Painting was the only thing going on there. It took forever because I wanted it to be perfect for you."

Rachel just stared. She didn't know what to say. She had always thought Derek was a good man, but had also learned at an early age that people lied. She had seen men turn on the tears and lie through their teeth a hundred times to her mother. She didn't know what to think. Her fear of being made a fool of paralyzed her.

"When I came to your apartment that day to surprise you, I had the portrait with me. I couldn't wait until the weekend to give it to you. It's still in my old closet at my parents' house. I could never look at it, but I could also never throw it away."

Rachel felt like she was frozen in place. They sat there staring at the floor together until they heard Grace coming through the door.

Derek took that as his cue to leave and stood up, wiping the tears from his face as he walked toward the door.

"Hi, Mrs. Stevens. Can I help you with those?" He took the bags she was carrying as she gave a quizzical look to Rachel. Rachel shrugged and mouthed, "Tell you later."

"Thank you, Derek. How is your dad?"

"He's much better and happy to be home. He's very appreciative of the prayers and cards. He said the food from the people of Hideaway saved his life when his only other option was hospital food."

He took a last long look at Rachel, as if he were looking right through to her soul. "Can we finish this sometime?"

"Yes, I think that would be a good idea. If your number is still the same, I'll text you." She gave a weak smile as she thanked Him for coming and watched him close the door behind him.

She stood frozen, clutching her stomach with her head hung low. She felt her grandmother's hand on her back and turned into her embrace. She cried on her shoulder like she used to as a child.

Chapter 22

Derek's head was reeling when he walked down the steps of Rachel's house. He couldn't believe what he had just heard. *All these years, she thought I had cheated on her? She thought I would cheat?*

He drove down and parked by the lake to get his composure. He stared out at the surging grey water for a few minutes. The water always calmed him, but today it was no match for the storm raging inside of him.

She really thought I would cheat? He couldn't get the thought out of his head.

"Lord, what do I do with this? How could it be so easy for her to think the worst of me? She *knew* me. I thought she knew me better than anyone, but I guess she didn't know me at all." He immediately knew that wasn't true, but if anything, knowing that made it even worse.

"She *did* know me better than anyone and yet she tossed me aside over something some random stranger said. She didn't even give me a chance to defend myself or ask for an explanation. After the stories she told me about men cheating on her mother . . . She thought I was *like* them?"

He straightened up and wiped the tears off his face. "It doesn't matter anyway. She's got a boyfriend who she apparently trusts more than she trusted me. Maybe that's why she's with him. Ben wouldn't cheat on *anything*."

Nor would I.

"I'm going to find that painting and show her and I guess that will be it."

When he walked in the door of his parents' kitchen, his father was cutting an apple. He took one look at his son and knew something was very wrong.

"What is it?"

"I just came from Rachel's house." Ed's eyebrows raised and he set his knife down. "Oh?"

"I lost her over a misunderstanding and an assumption, Dad. What am I supposed to do with *that*?" Ed's face fell.

"Oh, son."

Derek sat and put his head in his hands. Ed poured a cup of coffee for each of them and sat down next to him.

"She thought I *cheated* on her. She thought I would do that. How could she think that?"

Ed pondered the thought for a long moment. "Derek, do you remember when Mitch first came back from Afghanistan? Remember how careful we had to be with sudden movements and loud noises? Heck, he had to watch football games alone at his place because having people suddenly raise their hands or yell triggered him.

"Maybe Rachel was triggered by the idea of cheating. She told us what things were like with her mom and how horrible it was for her to see her mom hurt so badly. Maybe it had nothing to do with you or reality, just like it had nothing to do with us or reality when Mitch was adjusting to life out of a war zone."

"You may be right. No wonder sure wouldn't talk to me."

"Son, I think the bigger question here isn't about explaining why Rachel thought that. The big question is this: Are you willing to forgive her? Are you willing to wipe the slate clean with her?"

Derek took a long moment to consider the answer. "I want to . . . I do. It doesn't matter anyway, though, because now she's with Ben Peterson."

"Unless she has a ring on her finger, it matters. I've seen her with Ben and she doesn't look at him the way she used to look at you. Tell me what happened today."

Derek told him about the conversation, starting with the chance meeting at the post office.

Ed looked thoughtful. "She's probably as shocked as you are about how that conversation went and you both have a lot to think about right now. I've recently retired from telling you what to do at the office, but I'm still your dad and you're in my kitchen, so I get to tell you what to do here." His voice and expression were gentle as he gave a sympathetic smile.

"I've watched you live under a dark cloud since you lost her and your heart broke, and my heart has broken *for* you. Heck, my heart has broken for *me*, too. I loved that girl. I still do. She was a part of this family and I thought she was going to be the mother of my grandchildren." He squeezed Derek's arm.

"You need to take some time to pray about this. God will help you to forgive her and will help you to figure out if you're willing to trust her with your heart again. She may need time to absorb what she found out today, too, and to realize you are telling her the truth. I've learned just how important it is to have the right person by your side when life gets tough. I can't imagine getting through what I've just been through with anyone other than your mother by my side.

"You've got the chance you've been praying for here, son. You need to figure out if you still want that chance, and while you're figuring it out you need to remember that people aren't perfect and they will let you down. Remember *I* recently let you down and you forgave me. The forgiveness is only the first step. If you decide that you do want another chance with her, do what you have to do to get it. What you had was special. *She's* special and true love is worth it." He patted Derek on the shoulder and started in the direction of Derek's old room.

"Let's go find that portrait."

Chapter 23

"Do you want to talk about it?" Grace had held Rachel and let her cry for a good five minutes before she spoke. Rachel nodded, wiped the tears from her eyes, and sat on the couch. She had never been more thankful for the ever-present box of Puffs.

"I decided to ask Derek why he cheated on me."

"And what did he say?"

Rachel dissolved into tears again. "He said he didn't. He said the girl Molly saw him with was a girl from his art class and they were trading time modeling for each other for projects they were working on. He said she was his model for a portrait he was making of *me.*"

"Do you believe him?"

Rachel just stared into the distance. "I don't know what to believe. He seemed genuinely shocked when I asked him, and he denied it as strongly as I've ever seen him deny anything. He looked positively *stricken.*"

"You know, you learned at a young age not to depend on people. You couldn't depend on your mom because she was in pain and depressed and had a hard time taking care of herself. You couldn't depend on your father because as much as you wished for it, he never showed up on your doorstep.

You could only depend on yourself. You could only *trust* yourself.

"From the time you came to live with me, I tried to show you that you could depend on me and tried to surround you with other trustworthy people. You started opening up to me and to Auntie Ev and Shelby and Brianna, and you learned to let people in. You became good at reading people and learned to trust your own judgment."

She paused and turned Rachel's face toward her. "I'm bringing this up because I want to remind you how good you are at reading people and their intentions. And with that in mind, do you think Derek is lying or telling the truth?"

"I think he's telling the truth." The admission brought a fresh wave of tears. "I think he's telling the truth, but I'm afraid to believe him."

Grace put her arms around her and held her. It felt to Rachel just like all those times when she was younger when she wanted to believe that her mom would get better or her dad would come for her.

Hoping and believing were terrifying acts for Rachel. The consequences of getting it wrong were too great.

Rachel was glad to have the distraction of work the next day. She felt like she'd been in a stupor all day. Spilling her guts to her grandmother, then to Brianna and Shelby, was exhausting; it was also freeing. It even felt good to let out the tears that she hated so much. They all encouraged her to continue the conversation with him as soon as possible. She needed more answers. Most of all, she needed to figure out if she believed him. They all carefully avoided giving their opinions, but she suspected they believed his story.

It felt surreal to send a text to his number, but she invited him to come back over that evening after work. Her grandmother had offered to stay upstairs so they would have privacy and had prayed over her, asking God to heal her heart and reveal truth to her.

Truth was a hard concept for Rachel. Those 10 years with her mother were the equivalent of graduate training in deceit. She'd watched her mother's boyfriends lie to her about where they spent their time or who they were with. She'd been lied to *by* her mother in her mother's failed attempt to protect her from the reality of their circumstances. Worst of all, she'd watched her mother lie to herself about her ability to fight an addiction that had come about through no fault of her own.

She wished she'd known her mother before the accident that left her with constant, horrible pain, which caused her to need narcotics to get through every day, which led to addiction. By all accounts, she was a strong, ambitious, capable person with a bright future ahead of her before that fateful day on that snowy freeway. By all accounts, she was a good mother before that day and was making a good life for herself and Rachel. But the pain and eventual depression all became too much and she couldn't take care of herself or her daughter.

Being raised in that environment for 10 years had one advantage: Rachel had become somewhat of a deception expert. And her expertise told her Derek was telling the truth.

Realizing Derek was telling the truth brought a whole new wave of sorrow over Rachel. If he was telling the truth, *she* was the one who destroyed everything. *She* had refused to talk to him. *She* had refused to even tell him why she was breaking up with him or give him a chance to give his side of the story. *She* had completely shut down and refused to allow Shelby, Brianna, or her grandmother to even mention giving him a chance to explain. It was *she* who needed to beg for forgiveness, not Derek.

The shame threatened to overwhelm her. She spent the afternoon praying that God would forgive her and that He would prepare Derek's heart to forgive her. She almost cancelled the meeting she had just scheduled with him, but decided she needed to be brave again and go through with it.

Chapter 24

Derek approached her door cautiously. He had spent the past 24 hours trying to figure out what he wanted and had prayed with Clayton late into the night. He knew he could forgive her, but wanted his reputation with her cleared of any wrongdoing.

He couldn't stand the idea that she thought he would hurt her like that, that she could think of him as that kind of person. He also couldn't stand the uncertainty that was plaguing him about any future possibilities with her. *Lord, please show her that I'm telling the truth. And please show me if another chance is even an option for either of us now.*

She opened the door and looked as beautiful as he'd ever seen her. He took in her eyes for a moment and studied the gold flecks he'd tried so hard to duplicate in the portrait; those eyes that he had seen only in his memories and dreams for three and a half years. She gave a nervous smile and let him in. Her eyes had a cloud in them that he had never seen and looked like he wasn't the only one crying into the night. *This doesn't look good.*

"I brought you something." He handed over the carefully wrapped package. It felt like he was offering the most fragile thing in the world. In a way, he was; he may as well have been handing her his heart and a blender.

"Oh, you didn't have t–" Realization flashed across her face as she looked up in surprise. "Is this the portrait?" She said it like she believed that it existed without needing proof. He allowed himself a glimmer of hope.

She held the package gingerly as she crossed to the chair and set it down against the antique coffee table. He followed and sat on the comfortable couch. His back threatened to have phantom pain as he remembered the old couch.

"Nice couch." They shared a nervous laugh.

"I poured you some cinnamon tea. 'Tis the season and all." She looked nervously at the package.

"Do you want to open it?"

"Okay. It's wrapped so beautifully."

"It took me almost as long to wrap it as it did to paint it." He wiped his suddenly sweaty palms on his pants as he watched her pick it up.

She carefully unwrapped it and gasped. Her hand flew to her mouth, shaking. Her eyes filled with tears. "Derek, it's beautiful."

He found himself staring at it too. He hadn't seen it since the day he wrapped it and took it to her over three and a half years ago. *Those eyes.* He had spent more time on her eyes than on any part of the portrait.

"That's the last piece of artwork I made."

"Are you serious?"

He gave her a crooked smile. "Well, life kind of took a turn after that painting. I didn't feel terribly inspired."

"Oh, Derek." Her eyes misted up again. She gently set the painting down and turned to face him.

"When I invited you here the other day, I had a hard time finding words to say what I needed to say. I wanted you to know how much you hurt me and I wanted you to admit what you had done and apologize. I thought that would give me closure. I never expected you to tell me that it was all a mistake, that it never happened." She drew in a shaky breath and he braced himself for the worst.

As she continued, her voice took on a level of sorrow that he had never heard from her. It made him hurt inside to hear it. "It was *my* mistake. *I'm* the one who owes *you* the apology. You tried to talk to me back then and I wouldn't listen or tell you why I was breaking up with you. I blamed you for stealing the past three and a half years from me, but it was *me* who did that to both of us. *I'm* the one who messed everything up. I didn't even give you a chance to explain." Her brown eyes vanished behind tears and he saw that her lack of faith in him pained her as much as it pained him. Seeing the depth of her remorse was almost too much for him to take.

"Derek, I'm so sorry. Can you ever forgive me?"

He didn't think; he just acted. He stood from the couch, took her by the hands, and pulled her from her chair in one fell swoop. He took her in his arms and held her close. She held him as tightly as he held her.

"I already have. Can you forgive me for not trying harder to talk to you?"

"You tried and I accused you of stalking me. I was awful to you." She cried into his shoulder.

"I know how badly you feel and I meant it when I said I've forgiven you, Rachel. It's *done*."

They stood there for a moment, locked in an embrace. They still fit together perfectly. He tried not to notice the smell of her strawberry shampoo or how right it felt to have her in his arms again. After all, she was dating another man. As much as he wanted another chance with her, he was not going to go about it the wrong way.

He stepped back. "I'm sorry if I overstepped there. I got overwhelmed. I've wanted to clear the air with you for three and a half years, and for the past 24 hours all I could think about was having you believe me."

"I got overwhelmed, too, and I've spent the past 24 hours praying that you would forgive me for thinking you could ever do something like that." She looked at the floor, then back at him. "I don't even know what to say now." She gave a weak laugh.

"I don't know what to say, either. I know what I *want* to say, but I'm trying to be a man of character here." His eyes twinkled as he gave her a half-smile.

She tilted her head. "Unless you've completely changed recently, I'm pretty sure you're still a man of character. What do you want to say?"

"I *want* to ask for another chance. Would a man of character ask a woman who is dating someone else for another chance after the air has been cleared between them? Because if I can do that and still be a man of character, then that's what I want to do."

She looked confused for a moment, then a smile formed on her lips.

"I'm not dating anyone else." *Jackpot!*

"What about Ben Peterson?"

"Ben is just a friend. Neither of us were ever interested in dating."

"Then can I have another chance?"

"You'll really give *me* another chance?" The tears started to form in her eyes even as she said it.

He answered by drawing her back into his arms and holding her as closely as possible. This time he allowed all of his senses to take in everything about her and he reveled in having her in his arms. This time his lips found hers as they had so many times before.

They still fit together perfectly too.

He forced himself to break the kiss. He was happy to see that she was as breathless as he was. "If I'm going to remain a man of character, we're going to have to sit on opposite ends of this room or call your grandmother down here to chaperone. I've wanted this for too long to have reliable self-control."

She stepped back and smiled at him, taking his hand in hers.

"Me too." She called up the stairs. "Grandma? Can you come down here please?"

Chapter 25

Rachel couldn't believe how fast time seemed to be moving all of a sudden. It didn't seem real that it had only been a few days since she and Derek had reunited.

They had talked for hours each night and they took every opportunity to spend time together again. They had three and a half years of life to catch up on, and whether they were sitting in her living room, a warm car looking at the cold lake, or a corner booth at the Bayshore Diner, they did their best not to leave anything out. The thrill of being with him again and the gratitude for being forgiven for such a failure were overwhelming at times. It was almost impossible to focus on work or to take the smile off her face.

They had agreed to take things slowly so they could get to know each other again, but it felt like an impossible task for Rachel. It was as if the past three and a half years hadn't happened and they were right back in sync with each other.

They had decided to go separately to the annual caroling party at Summit Mountain as part of the taking-things-slow plan. It helped that Brianna and Shelby had both finally gotten home and they wanted to spend time with her, too. Their time was mostly spent giggling and whispering about him, but still.

She always looked forward to the annual event and enjoyed every minute of it. Even though it was a big affair taking up several rooms, it didn't overwhelm her like some events. She was always so focused on all the beautiful trees and twinkle lights and fresh garlands and Christmassy feel that it distracted her from the crowds. The chorus that led the carols was made up of local high school and college students who sang like angels and they were the finishing touch on the festive environment that was created there.

It was wonderful to get to see Derek's family outside of a hospital room and with no cloud hanging over the discussion. It was even more wonderful that they weren't mad at her.

"We're so happy to have you back, Rachel; we've missed you." Carol's smile showed she meant it. "And Derek was in a dark place for a long time, but we have him back now, too. Now that we have Ed back and Derek back and you back, we need to schedule a family game night."

Derek gave her a squeeze and a wicked grin that suggested that he was thinking the same thing she was: *Footsies is back!*

On the way back to Hideaway, Rachel, Brianna, and Shelby were giggling like schoolgirls as they threw around ideas about what Rachel could give to Derek for Christmas. Somehow, the quiet and studious Rachel, the bubbly and athletic Shelby, and the strong-willed and activistic Brianna all acted like 12-year-olds when they got together.

"Get him a time machine."

"A wedding veil."

"Handcuffs so he can make you sit still and listen next time there's a misunderstanding."

"Or for other things after you make use of the wedding veil." That one sent them all into such giggle fits that they could hardly breathe.

When they got the silliness out of their systems, she was still perplexed. She wanted to do something extra special to show how thankful she was that Derek forgave her and didn't make her pay for her awful mistake.

Brianna was direct. "Seriously, Rachel, he has *you*. You're all he wants; you're all he *ever* wanted. He was walking on air tonight at the party. You two did a pretty good job of playing down the fact that you're back together, but he couldn't stop staring at you and smiling all night."

Shelby looked so tired, but she was summoning up all of her energy to have girlfriend time. "She's right. Don't stress yourself. He has his gift. So do you. Just enjoy it."

"I'm the one who got the gift. He just acted like it was nothing to forgive me for messing everything up. He's amazing. I hurt him and he's still amazing."

Brianna looked at her intently. "Rachel, I want you to listen to me, ok? He has never made you pay for doing something wrong. He has always forgiven and moved on. It's who he is.

There is no other shoe to drop here. He just loves you. It's ok to trust that, accept the grace given, and *enjoy* it."

"I have the best friends in the whole world." She put her hand out so they could squeeze it together.

They made plans to see each other a few days later as she dropped them off. Shelby would be out of commission for at least a couple of days after the long drive up from Tennessee and the party. Brianna was planning on spending as much time as she could with her little niece Lily and getting to know Emily, since Joe and Emily had started dating and it seemed to be getting serious quickly. She was a protective sister and wanted to make sure the good things she'd heard about Emily were true.

For her part, Rachel had to figure out what to do for Christmas for Derek and would need time to think and make something happen.

Chapter 26

Derek was feeling better than he had in years. Up until a week ago, he had been dreading this Christmas season even more than the last three.

He hadn't even dreaded the first one after he and Rachel broke up; he just stumbled through it in a daze. He was still so depressed at that point, especially because he should have been getting ready for his wedding, that he avoided all activities other than work.

The second one wasn't much better. He just avoided all holiday activities, opting instead to stay at home and watch TV. He'd spent Christmas Day with his family and tried to be festive, but it was all an act; a bad one, at that.

Last year he and Clayton conspired to convince their parents to go to Florida as a family for Christmas so that he didn't have to be in town for it. He had long since figured out that it was actually the family conspiring to get *him* out of town, not the other way around. When he first realized that he had been manipulated, he was upset, but it didn't take long to realize that it was an act of love meant to save his pride. They had all enjoyed the sunshine and warmth, but it didn't feel like Christmas to any of them being away from their tiny town and the snow and their friends.

Now that he and Rachel were back together, he planned to enjoy every snowflake and every twinkle light. He had done just that at the party at Summit Mountain a couple of nights before. Carols sounded more melodic and eggnog tasted sweeter and the tree was more fragrant this year.

Being at the party separately and trying to keep their reunion low key so as to not send too many tongues wagging or having to answer questions was somewhat torturous, but he managed to spend moments with her here and there. He had immediately regretted their agreement to take things slowly.

He wanted to dance in the street and shout from the rooftops. He wanted the world to know that she was his again and that all was well.

He had a hard time concentrating on anything at work, but since it was Christmas, business was slow and everyone in the office was either already on vacation or thinking about vacation. No one noticed that his head was in the clouds except his father and brother, who were both thrilled about the reason why.

He tried to control the spring in his step as he climbed the stairs of Rachel's porch. The fresh snowfall had left them slightly slippery and he had no intention of breaking his neck before celebrating Christmas with her. He quickly cleared off the porch steps and sprinkled some sand on them before knocking on the door.

Rachel was still upstairs when he arrived, but Grace showed him in with a warm smile. She had her hands full of decorations, so she gestured with her head toward the desk where there was a manila envelope with insurance documents for him to take home after dinner. *We take full-service to a whole new level at the Cooper Agency.*

He stuffed the large packet into the side of a bag she'd given him that was loaded with canned goods for his church's food drive and helped her arrange the garland above her carved mantle.

"It's good to have you back in this room, Derek. And it's good to have the light back in Rachel's eyes. I'm glad you were able to get to the truth of things and forgive her and find your way back to each other."

"Me too. It's an answer to prayer, for sure. I begged God for another chance with her and I'm not going to blow it."

He looked up as she came downstairs and he watched every step. She was wearing a deep green sweater dress that flattered her eyes and her soft curves. The lip gloss she was wearing made him wish he could steal a quick kiss or 10 before dinner. He realized he was grinning like an idiot and started to feel embarrassed, but then realized that Rachel was grinning too.

Grace looked back and forth between them. "Oh, to be young and in love." He startled at her use of the word 'love', but there was no point in denying it. "Guilty." He winked at Grace.

Rachel blushed. She greeted him with a quick hug and he kissed her cheek, the second-best spot on her face for such things. "You look beautiful."

Grace headed for the stairs. "Goodnight, you two. You behave yourselves now." She gave a final smile before going up to her room.

Derek looked at Rachel. "I thought we were all having dinner together."

"*We* are having dinner together. *She* is giving us space."

"I like space with you. Can I help you set the table?"

"No, but you can spread the blanket on the floor in front of the fireplace. We're having a picnic."

When he got home that night, he decided to take a quick look at the insurance documents that Grace had sent with him to make sure everything was in order. He was actually enjoying his job for the first time, now that they had specific roles spelled out and were working as a team to run the agency.

When he pulled the packet of paper out, he realized he must have picked up the wrong one. It was a book manuscript. Rachel had mentioned she was doing some editing for someone. As he started to put it back in the envelope, the words on the page caught his attention:

Clyde Wainwright stood and surveyed what was left of his farm. The Confederate soldiers had done a good job of torching the place, but thanks to God and a tip from one of the scouts, all of the runaway slaves he had been housing in his cellar and attic had long since gone. He and his family had risked their own lives to carry on as if nothing had changed, and it had paid off. Several families escaped further north to start new lives in freedom, and the Wainwrights knew they had done the Lord's work.

The mound of ashes grew before his eyes, but as the last pieces of the house burned against the backdrop of the early morning sunrise, he smiled wryly. "We'll start rebuilding in the morning."

Derek was riveted as he read on. He could smell the fire burning and see the smoke rising in front of the morning sun. He continued reading until the lure of the box in his garage got the best of him and he pulled out his paints.

Chapter 27

Rachel was frantic. She couldn't find her manuscript anywhere. She was sure she had laid it on the desk in the front room, but it had vanished. Asking her grandmother about it would mean she had to actually tell her of its existence. She wasn't ready to share it yet, even with her grandma.

"What are you looking for, dear?

"Oh, I left something on this desk and can't seem to find it. Just some work stuff."

Her grandmother started picking up items to help. "Wait, this is the envelope Derek was supposed to take last night. I hope he didn't take your work stuff by accident."

Rachel felt the blood drain right out of her. *What if he read it?* She felt a rush of panic. She had to get it back. Immediately.

She sent a text to Derek saying she thought he may have grabbed the wrong envelope and that she would bring over the right one on her way to work. She then sent a second text asking him not to look in the envelope he had with him.

She rushed out the door as quickly as she could. She felt anxious and tried to talk herself down. *This is what happens when secrets come out of closets and hidden files in computers.*

"What if he reads it? What if he figures out I wrote it? I'm so glad I didn't print a title page. Oh, Lord, please fix this. Please don't let Derek read it or figure out that I wrote it."

She slowed the car way down as she got closer to his place. She had never been there, but had the address and knew it was a small cottage in the alley behind a bigger home on Evergreen Avenue. Back in days gone by, families would move into the cottages in the summer and rent out their big homes to rich families from Chicago. Now, some people used the cottages as regular rental properties, renting to locals rather than tourists.

She slowed more than she needed to, giving herself another moment to get her breathing under control and give the appearance of normalcy. Sanity felt just out of reach.

"Okay, I can pull this off. It's just some work stuff, no big deal. Not something that came out of my head or something that's important to me. Just run-of-the-mill, not-a-big-deal-yet-important work stuff."

She was still shaking on the inside when she knocked on his door. When he opened the door he was freshly shaven and ready to go to work, but his red eyes suggested he hadn't slept much. He looked at her sheepishly and kissed her on the cheek as Brutus fought for her attention.

"Derek, are you ok?"

"Yes, I was just up late. Do you have a minute for coffee? I need to tell you something."

"Um, ok. Can I switch out the envelopes first so I don't forget?" *Act casual. You'll make the switch and drink your coffee and it will all be fine. Just breathe.*

He handed her the envelope and she handed him the one she brought. *Home free. Now I can exhale and enjoy coffee and bonus time with him.*

She wrapped her free arm around Derek's waist. "Can I get a real 'good morning' kiss with that cup of coffee now? Brutie is the only one who's really given me kisses this morning." She grinned as she pulled him in for a quick peck on the lips. "Good morning."

"Good morning." He looked away as he poured her coffee and asked her to sit at the tiny table in his kitchen. "So we've talked about not having any secrets or misunderstandings, right? Well, I have a confession to make."

Oh no. For the second time in an hour, she felt the blood drain from her face. She was glad she was sitting down this time.

"I know what's in that envelope. I pulled the papers out last night thinking they were the insurance documents. By the time I realized what they were, it was too late. I read the first few sentences and couldn't stop. This morning when I got your text, I realized that you *really* didn't want them to be read."

He read it. No! Wait, did he say he couldn't stop?

He continued as he stood up from the table. "Rach, your friend's writing is really good. I was up until 4:00 am because of it. Well, I read until 2:00 and then I had to stop to do something. Will you come in here for a minute?" *It's ok. He thinks it's your friend's writing. It's ok.*

She stood on wobbly legs and followed him into the living room, where he had spread a tarp on the floor and set up his easel. On the easel was a painting of Clyde Wainwright's burning house.

She gasped as her hands flew to her face. "Oh my gosh, it's Clyde's house. It's exactly as it was in my mind." She winced and hoped he didn't catch her slip of the tongue.

"That's what I mean! This is how it was in my mind when I was reading it, too. It's exactly as it was on the *page*. That's what I mean about your friend's writing. This book is really good."

Chapter 28

Derek turned away from the painting to look at Rachel in his excitement. She looked like she had seen a ghost. It dawned on him that there was another reason she was so adamant that he not read the book.

"Wait. Rachel, did *you* write this book?"

Her words were barely a whisper as she stared at the painting. "I wrote it." She sat down on the couch as if she were trying to avoid passing out.

He sat next to her and hugged her, and Brutus took up residence on her other side. "Honey, it's wonderful. You're a talented writer."

"It's been my secret project for years. I never wanted anyone to know about it."

Oh, no. I blew it. "Rachel, I'm so sorry. I had no idea it was a secret." She didn't move. *Well, at least she's not leaving.*

"Rachel? I'm really sorry." He felt like the world's biggest toad. It had always frightened him when Rachel shut down like this. He asked God to help her and to give him words that wouldn't make it worse. She shifted, and instead of moving away from him like she used to do, she settled in under his arm and let him hold her close. *Thank You, Jesus.*

"Grandma and Shelby and Brianna don't even know about this book. They don't know about *any* of my books."

"*Books*? Plural? There are more?"

She looked at him and a flash of what looked like relief washed across her face. "Yes. We're sharing secrets and trusting each other again, so I'll tell you what the others don't know. I started writing books after we broke up. It was a good distraction from — you know. I've been selling them under a pseudonym since then. But I've just written what I thought people wanted to read and written like others do. Those don't feel like my books. This book is different; *this* feels like mine. I never planned to publish it, so I wrote what *I* wanted to write, not what I thought someone else wanted. That's why until a week ago, this was in a box in the back of my closet."

"Rach, I know it's scary to share your creation with the world. That's how I felt when I brought you in to see the painting. It's *really* how I felt when I gave you the portrait. It's a part of *me* on that canvas, just like it's a part of *you* on the pages of that book."

"It feels good to tell you and I love that you understand. I *really* love that you're painting again. I can't believe you painted Clyde's house so perfectly." She smiled and leaned her head on his shoulder.

He rested his head on hers. "I'm inspired again. I'm sorry for reading without your blessing. Thank you for telling me about the other books. Your secret is safe with me. But will you consider publishing this? I'm not sure if I told you, but it's *really* good."

She got a sparkle in her eye as she looked up at him. "Good enough that I can keep the painting?"

Chapter 29

Rachel didn't know how to feel. It had been two days since she had told Derek about her secret writing career. It was wonderful to let him in on it and talk to him about it, but it still left her feeling unsettled. Sharing it with anyone, even him, was new territory for her.

"Lord, how do I know if he said he thought it was good just to make me feel happy?"

She wondered if others had as hard a time accepting compliments on their important works as she did. She wondered if others had as hard a time believing people as she did. She thought back to the conversation she'd had with her grandmother about Derek and her mother. *Do I believe he's telling the truth?*

She realized she did. He had no agenda. He had loved the book when he thought someone else wrote it.

He saw Clyde's house exactly as I saw it. She decided that it was time for another brave act.

Chapter 30

Derek folded up the tarp and smiled. It had only been three days of being back to painting again, and it was hard to put his supplies away. Having a date with Rachel made it easier. He shook his head. *This is surreal. It's Friday night and I have a date with Rachel. This will definitely be better than my last trip to the Birchwood Inn.*

It was even more surreal to think that he was going to be spending Christmas with her. Having Rachel back and his family back and his life back made him feel like there was no present on earth that could improve on things. He had everything he needed and everything he wanted and he felt like himself again.

He stepped back and looked at the painting he was working on for his parents for Christmas. It was a picture of the river where they used to go camping as a family when he and Clayton were kids. There were such good memories there and it seemed like the perfect painting to give to them this year. He was pleased with the way it was turning out and was shocked that he didn't feel rusty after his three and a half year break. *All I needed was Rachel's writing and Clyde Wainwright's burning house. I'm back, baby!*

Chapter 31

Rachel picked up the house phone, expecting to hear Evelyn's voice. "Rachel? It's Mom." Something sounded very different and she almost didn't recognize her voice.

It was always a surprise to hear from her mother, and Rachel reflexively felt the tension in her stomach and chest. "Hi, Mom."

"I wanted to wish you an early Merry Christmas. I know you'll probably be busy in a few days."

"Thank you. Merry Christmas to you, too." *She actually sounds good.*

"How are you doing, sweetheart? Are you having a nice holiday season?"

"Sure. The town is doing all the usual stuff, so it's been busy and fun. We went to the caroling party at Summit Mountain the other night, which was beautiful as always, and Auntie Ev's tree trimming party is tomorrow night. What about you, Mom? Where are you living?" She kicked herself for asking the question that so often got avoided.

There was silence on the other end of the phone for a moment.

"I'm in a treatment center in Kentucky. I know you've heard that before, but this one is different. *I'm* different. I'm in a special program for people who have chronic pain and who got hooked on narcotics because of it. They use nutrition and all sorts of alternative treatments that work with the pain and addiction and different types of psychotherapy to help with sorting out all of the emotional and psychological baggage. It's really helping and I feel better than I have in years."

Rachel was afraid to get excited. Her mother sounded better than she had in a long time, and it was a huge change for her to use the word 'addiction', but Rachel knew from painful experience that getting her hopes up was risky. "That's good, Mom. I hope they can help you there."

"I didn't want to tell you that I was here until I had gotten through Phases I and II of the program; that's why I didn't mention it when we talked a few months ago. I've never gotten through this far before and I didn't want to get your hopes up if I wasn't going to do it. I've been here for ten months and I'm *doing it* this time, Rachel. I almost didn't tell you where I was when you asked because I wanted to surprise you with a year completed, but I would rather be honest with you . . . even when it spoils surprises." She laughed nervously.

"I'm glad you told me then." D*id she say ten months?* "That's a wonderful surprise, Mom. I'm happy for you and I'll be praying that this will be the one that works this time."

"Thank you. I'll take all the prayers I can get. I've sure been praying enough of my own." *Really?*

Rachel could tell her mother was fighting tears just as she was as she continued. "Well, I know that you're busy, so I'll let you go. I just wanted to wish you a Merry Christmas. Will you tell Grandma that I love her and that I'll call her soon?"

"I will. She'll be glad you're safe and getting help. Merry Christmas, Mom. I'm– I'm glad you called. And congratulations. I love you."

She heard her mother's breath catch. "I love you too, sweetheart."

She hung up the phone and prayed, "Lord, please help her. Please send whatever she needs to get better. I want to have hope for her even though it's scary."

It was so nice to be able to talk to Derek about her phone call with her mother at dinner. He had always been a good listener and had given her perspective on things.

"She's been there for *ten months?* Wow, that's a long time for her. What was the most time she spent in a place before?"

"Six weeks. She always said the pain had gotten to be too much and she went back to her regular doctors for more meds. It's scary to hope, but she sounded so different. I almost didn't recognize her voice when she called. It sounded *strong*. It sounded like she wasn't on anything. Hope is still scary, though."

Derek took her hand and squeezed it. "Rachel, the fact that we're sitting here together on a date, playing footsies under the table, and discussing our daily lives is proof that all things are possible. There's always hope." He paused, then continued. "What about the forgiveness part with her? You know, we wouldn't be sitting here together if you hadn't forgiven me. You weren't willing to sit down and talk with me until you forgave me, and if that hadn't happened, we wouldn't have gotten the misunderstanding out and cleared the air between us. Have you forgiven her?"

"I have. But I need to take the next step that you took with me. We wouldn't be here tonight if you hadn't risked letting me in again after I hurt you so badly. I'm so grateful for getting another chance after what I did and I need to give her another chance too. I need to be brave and hope."

"You can do it and you know God will help you. And I'm here to help you, too." He smiled and kissed her hand just as the waiter brought their food.

As he prayed for their meal, he included her mother's treatment and prayed for Rachel's courage to hope.

Oh, Lord, I've missed this. Thank You for giving us another chance. Please give my mom another chance. Please heal her and bring her back to me like You brought Derek back to me.

Chapter 32

Derek was glad he'd convinced Rachel to throw caution to the wind and go together to Evelyn's tree trimming party. He was failing miserably at taking things slowly and he didn't care.

He'd never stopped loving Rachel and in the short time they'd been back together, his love had multiplied. The relationship was better than it ever was, now that they'd both matured enough to be more direct and open with each other. Going through the painful process of being hurt and forgiving had taken the relationship to a deeper level than he'd ever experienced.

She took his breath away, as usual, when he picked her up. He still couldn't believe she was next to him in his car, on their way to a party together, like no time had interrupted things.

"I think you need to pinch me. Actually, don't; if I'm dreaming, I don't want to wake up. Plus, you're stronger than you look."

She just laughed. "I won't pinch you if you don't pinch me. I like our shared dream. And I'm glad you convinced me to go together to the party. I like having the extra alone time with you on the short drive and I don't care if people are talking about us."

"I like alone time with you, too. Maybe we should skip the party." He winked in her direction. "On second thought, that might be dangerous, because I like alone time with you a little *too* much. The party it is."

"The party it is. The room full of people it is."

"Unless, of course, you sneak off to the library."

"You know me too well."

Chapter 33

Rachel, Shelby, and Brianna gathered up the boxes from the ornaments after the tree was completely decorated and placed them neatly into the appropriate boxes so that Derek and Mitch could whisk them away to the attic. Derek plopped a kiss on Rachel's cheek before heading upstairs.

Brianna rolled her eyes at Rachel. "Between you two and my brother and Emily, I've never seen so many googly eyes in one room."

"Sorry. Speaking of googly eyes, I thought Mr. Wonderful was coming up for the party and to stay for a couple of days."

"He called this morning and said he was locked in by a snowstorm in Ohio. When he said it, I wasn't even a little bit disappointed. You know what that means; I think it's time to say goodbye to that one."

Shelby put her arm around Brianna. "I'm sorry; I was hoping that would work out for you. Maybe now that Rachel is done with Ben, you could borrow him." Shelby could barely get the sentence out before giggling. Brianna let out a laugh and jabbed her friend in the ribs.

"The sparks I've been seeing tonight only confirm my decision. I'm not settling. I want googly eyes, too."

"Good. And we didn't want you moving to Ohio either. That's way too far away. And it's *Ohio*. People who graduate from Michigan should never move to Ohio."

"Is this a new route you're taking? My house is just a few blocks from Evelyn's, you know." She gave the same teasing look as she used to give him when he did that, as if she minded the longer drive.

"I'm trying out a new route to give me more time with my date."

"You know I've always liked taking the long way around town with you and I like having more time alone after having to be with all those people tonight. Christmas parties take a lot out of introverts, you know."

"I know." He pulled into a parking spot by the beach. "I'm glad we went together tonight. It was really fun to be back at Evelyn's again."

"She told me she was glad to have you back there, too. She's very happy for us."

"I'm happy for us, too. I know we're taking things slow, but we're also being completely honest and I feel like I'm holding something back." She held her breath on reflex as he took her hands.

"Rachel, I never stopped loving you and I love you more now than I ever have. I just had to tell you that. I don't want to rush things or push you, but it felt weird not to say that to you."

"I love you, too, Derek!" She leaned over and threw her arms around his neck. "As much as I tried to stop loving you, it never worked and I never stopped either. I don't know why I thought I had to hold back from telling you that, too, but I'm glad you said it."

They sealed it with a kiss, of course, as they sealed most statements.

Chapter 34

Derek locked the door to the office and sighed. No work for almost two weeks. There was no point in keeping the agency open when the clients were on vacation, so they were officially off the clock.

It was actually his father's idea to close the office at noon on Christmas Eve and keep it closed until January 5th. Since his release from the hospital, he had kept his promise to not let the business run him anymore. The way the days fell on the calendar this year cooperated nicely with his new attitude and would give them a nice long break.

Rachel and Grace had invited his family to Christmas Eve dinner at their house, then to the candlelight service at their church, First Community. The beautiful old church with the tall steeple was his favorite setting for a candlelight Christmas Eve service. It would be nice to be in church on Christmas Eve again. It would be nice to really celebrate Christmas again. His parents had invited Rachel and Grace to their house for Christmas dinner, too, so everything was falling back into place, where it belonged.

His Christmas present for Rachel had finally arrived at his house and he needed to find a way to wrap it nicely for her and get over to her house before everyone showed up for dinner. He and her grandmother had made arrangements so that he and Rachel would have some alone time before everyone got there, but he didn't have a second to spare.

When he arrived on her doorstep, she was waiting and looking stunning. She had on a new, to him at least, winter white dress and had curled her hair so it framed her face softly. He set decorum aside and took her into his arms and kissed her when he crossed the threshold. "Merry Christmas."

"Merry Christmas. Is this why you got my grandma out of the house this afternoon?" She gave him a coy smile.

"No. This is." He handed her the package as he stepped into the room and closed the door. "I couldn't give this to you in front of the others without blowing your secret."

She unwrapped the box to reveal the leather manuscript satchel and smiled. "It's beautiful. And it has a little lock!"

"That's so nosy people can't peek at your work before you're ready anymore."

She laughed as she caressed the satchel. "I love it. And the leather is so soft."

"Just promise me you'll let me read everything you write and that you'll keep praying about publishing the other ones, the *real* ones."

"I promise. And speaking of that, I wanted to give you your gift without prying eyes around too."

She reached for a box under the tree with his name. He opened it and inhaled sharply. "What? Rachel, it's your book! With my painting on the cover!"

"I decided to self-publish, like I did with my other books, but I put my own name on it this time. I gathered up courage that you gave me and did it. Then I ordered a rush hard copy. Read the dedication."

To Derek, the man of my dreams and love of my life who encourages me to be more than I ever thought I could be.

"Wow. Your gift completely beat mine."

She laughed and shrugged. "Sorry."

He had planned to hold off for a few days for his other surprise for her, but decided he was done holding off.

"Hmm, I think I might be able to beat it. Where is your portrait?"

"Grandma insisted on putting it up by the Christmas tree for the holidays."

He could hardly contain himself as he walked over to the wall and carefully took the picture down. He stood in front of the Christmas tree and turned toward her with the back of the portrait facing her. He grinned and tried to will away the tears that wanted to form in his eyes as he tapped his finger, pointing to the small wood square box on the inside of the frame. He was glad she hadn't noticed it there before.

She reached out and pulled the box from the frame with shaking hands and looked up at him. She was losing her own battle with tears as he put the frame back and took the box from her hand. "Allow me."

He opened the box, got down on one knee, and held the ring out to her. "Rachel, I love you and want to spend the rest of my life with you. Will you please forget this ridiculous idea about taking things slow and marry me?"

"Of course I will! I'll marry you anytime, anywhere."

He took her hand as he stood and placed the ring on her finger, staring at it when it was in place to make sure it was real.

"I've been waiting three and a half years to do that."

"You mean back then you were going to propose?"

"Yes. But that wasn't God's timing for us; this is. We both had some growing to do and He used that time to do important things in us." He drew her into his arms and wiped away the tear that was running down her cheek. "I know we said we were going to take things slow before, but I asked for permission from God and from your grandma to do this now."

He gave a sly grin. "Plus, I lied when I said I thought we should take things slow."

Her grin matched his. "So did I."

"How do you feel about a February wedding like we always planned?"

"I feel like February is a long time away." They laughed together and she continued as she laced her fingers through his hair. "I think February is *perfect*. Can we still rent a little cabin at Summit Mountain like we always planned? One with a big enough floor for picnics in front of the fireplace?"

"I put the deposit down today."

They got so caught up in the kisses that followed that they didn't hear their family members come in through the front door. Ed cleared his throat. "It looks like someone started the celebrations without us!" Everyone laughed together and Derek took Rachel's hand to cover up the ring. He looked at her to get the go-ahead and when she smiled and gave him a nod, he lifted her hand to show them.

"We're celebrating a very short engagement here."

Everyone cheered and came in to deliver hugs and congratulations to the happy couple. Carole looked at the ring and smiled at Rachel with tears in her eyes. "I've been praying for four years that the next time I saw my mother's ring, it would be on your hand." *Once again, Mother knows best.*

About the Author

Katherine Karrol is both a fan and an author of lighthearted, sweet, clean Christian romance stories. Because she does not possess the ability or desire to put a good book down and generally reads them in one sitting, she writes books that can be read in the same way.

Her books are meant to entertain and even possibly inspire the reader to take chances, trust God, and laugh at life as much as possible. The people she interacts with in her professional life have absolutely no idea that she writes these books, so by reading this, you agree to keep her secret.

If you would like to contact her to share your favorite character or share which actors you were picturing as you were reading, you can follow her on Facebook and Instagram or email her at KatherineKarrol@gmail.com.

About the Summit County Series

The Summit County Series is a group of standalone books that can be read singly, but those who read all of them in order will get a little extra something out of them as they see the characters and stories they've read about previously continue. It is set in a small town in Northern Michigan, where everyone knows everyone else, so the same characters and places will make cameos or possibly show up in significant roles in multiple books.

This series is near and dear to the author's heart because she spends as much time as possible in places that look an awful lot like the places in Summit County. She is certain that the people who know her and/or live in the area that inspired Summit County will think characters and situations are based on them or their neighbors (or even on her) and she assures them that they are not. The characters and stories are merely figments of her imagination. Well, except for Jesus. He's totally real.

35282141R00081

Made in the USA
Columbia, SC
20 November 2018